Parallel Carousel

Parallel Carousel

Short Stories & Poems

SAIRA KHAN

iUniverse, Inc.
New York Bloomington

Parallel Carousel
Short Stories & Poems

iUniverse books may be ordered through booksellers or by contacting:

iUniverse
1663 Liberty Drive
Bloomington, IN 47403
www.iuniverse.com
1-800-Authors (1-800-288-4677)

ISBN: 978-1-4502-3461-0 (pbk)
ISBN: 978-1-4502-3462-7 (ebk)

Printed in the United States of America

iUniverse rev. date: 8/4/2010

Contents

I. POEMS

I.
POEMS

Parallel Carousel

Once upon a world, before this world of love abound,
I stepped into a distant land. Somehow near,
Yet far. It was a mesmerising universe within a fairground.
I walked slowly in its dim light, gripped by fear,
Stepping past the stalls selling sight and sound.
Passing a grotesque stooped figure ringing his bell.
I scurried past the vicious bartering of the fairground
To come upon a mystical Carousel.
And so I took flight, nymph-like, through the crowd
Of shouting pixies and dwarfs. And then I heard that sound.

Oh, that I could capture the moment of terror that gripped me
When I heard that ominous waltz from the Carousel!
I moved slowly forward until I saw before me more clearly
Some terrible creation of heaven and beautiful gift from hell.
I carried on towards the spinning creatures
Somehow spinning through the lights in my mind.
Ancient animals with laughing eyes yet menacing features,
A more terrifying sight I have yet to find.
And as the vibrations echoed through earth and sea
The griffins, horses and playful dragons smiled down on me.

Suddenly I heard a crash and the poles dropped down,
The maniacal creatures now free to consume my sorry state.
But they carried on moving in circles, a merry-go-round,
Quietly accepting their selves and their monotonous fate.
And what was to be my fate in this magical tale?
I slowly stepped onto the plinth of the carousel and began the dance.
My eyes now red, like the creatures, with sharp claws and a tail,
And I walked around on all fours in some dreamlike trance.
There I was. Trapped in the never ending cycle of the mystical carousel.
Now close to myself, my lord, my heaven, my hell.

Die in the Happy Sky

I often wondered what it is that I need
To make a story come to life.
If only I could be the shiny seed
That grows above the strife.
That king, that queen, on the muddy throne,
Can see the euphoria has gone.
So I would sing, and louder sing,
For the happiness of our king.

Can you hear the goodness creep through the cracks?
Is this the scene I must live to see?
Close your doors and then call back
That sweet and bitter honey bee.
The sagacious rogue comes to mind
Who, with knowledge, has made me blind.
So I run, and faster run,
Only to get burnt by the loving sun.

The old man that destroyed me
Has slouched back to reclaim his heart.
His words more harmful than an angry sea
When, from the pain, they could not part.
He comes back to start the flame,
He wants to hurt me again and again.
So I fly, and higher fly,
Only to die in the happy sky.

Love Story

Love was true. True?
As true as gold to a pauper.
Love is; a fable, so full of life.
Its home is where players play.
A stage. Like Truth and Honesty.
Where music emanates from instruments
Though all claim it's from the heart.

Birds disturb my thoughts with infernal singing,
It is not music to my ears, not now.
Cynicism, my best friend, walks beside me.
His whispers calm my agitated state.

Of late I have felt comfort in the blackness
Surrounding me, trapping me inside.
The sun, the stars, the moon
Now pester me with their brightness.

Rivers may dry up, the Sun may melt,
And Love will still be a mere play
For all to see, and dream to have.
So sting the blessed bee my friend, and run!

Emotions guide me across my worst fears,
I scorn my past delusions and discard my tears.
The lascivious black mist still engulfs the air.
There is no love, it was never there.

Spring Awakening

The Summer's call to nature.
A time shift to tease the world out from Winter's solitude.
The earth is blessed, bathed in joyous light.
The trees look taller now, as do I.
An expanse of fields spreads before me.
Tiny specks of white on a blanket of green,
The cold warmth of a spring awakening.

The farmer

I sow seeds of time,
I toil in the fields of my father.
A quiet existence is mine
With only my soul left to barter.

You can find me in the shadows
And within the sacred realms of the heavenly mist.
A lone bird flying over the glorious meadows;
In the spaces between is where I serenely exist.

Scholar of Strife

He sits quietly at his desk, pen in hand,
Ready to be told another's tale of woe.
Yet the sadness inside him is more than he can stand
So he lets his pen trace over his sorrow.

They come and go and notice nothing
But the undivided attention of this scholar of strife.
They talk, they cry, his smile endearing
Them to seek his counsel throughout their life.

Yet no seed plants he into the soil,
No tangible object made for all to see.
Nothing he can show as evidence of his toil
As his words escape into the air, flying free.

So he adjusts his tie, runs his fingers over his suit.
He walks through the village he ran through as a boy
And looks at the farmer, his overalls and sodden boot,
Secretly wishing he was him, and for nature's joy.

And now times are changing, he cannot keep pace
With the global market that has kicked open the door.
He sinks lower in esteem, his haggard face
Now ignored by his clients and remembered no more.

Maybe if his words were seeds
They would grow in full view, tall and strong.
Now he feels he has nothing anyone needs,
And perhaps he knew this all along.

My Forgotten Home

Let me take you beyond the furthest mountain
To a place past hope and love.
Let me take you to an empty fountain
To a place below, with no above.

The birds flew freely here
In the hallowed twilight sky.
A setting so distant from sadness and fear.
Small hills and holy rye.

There was not one king in the kingdom,
Just kings and queens in heart.
Not one star had shone
But a constellation that would never part.

Look, and you will find my forgotten house
That, on this land, proudly stood.
Nothing there now, not a spider or mouse.
Just straw, bricks and wood.

The glass shattered when the house was sold
And my tears seeped into the walls.
With the lights now gone and the fireplace cold,
Nobody can hear my heart with its calls.

Prisoner

I cry inside. I do not want to be here.
My life ebbs away into the beautiful sea.
I remain imprisoned in this dungeon of fear,
A pathetic spectacle is all that is left of me.
I do not know how long I can last
In this fermenting container of hopelessness.
I am clinging to remnants of my glorious past
Lest they disintegrate into forgetfulness.
My Master whistles for me to come
Though talks politely to his other slaves.
So, I imagine I am the king's eldest son
Surrounded by princesses, officials and knaves,
And I talk to them with esteemed reverence and love
And they smile and raise me to a pedestal above.
But, alas, I awake from my reverie to see my lowly form
And the profound inequality which has become the norm.

I cry inside. My mind now my only salvation.
And yet, also the source of my unfathomable pain,
Which weaves through the small crevices of my elation
To remind me of my hell. But I must refrain
From instinct to hate those who laugh and jeer,
So I bow to my Master with my tattoed smile.
I must accept my position and perhaps steer
Towards a better future, yet I slave all the while.
I see those eyes, yet they do not see mine
And judge me inconsequential. They ignore my longing
To be home in whose bosom I would entwine.
But all I can do is obey, waiting. Always waiting.
Do they see me? If they do not see my mind
Do they see me at all? Or have I left them behind
As I swim away in my dreams, towards the sea.
Yes, in dreams I can truly live as was meant for me.

You love me

You tell me you love me,
You like me, you adore me.
You don't know how or why
You love me the way you do.

So much do you love me, you say,
That the moon turns away
From the brightness of my eyes.
So much, that flowers weep over
The exquisite colour of my lips.
So much, that the oak bows its head
To your love, which is so noble and beautiful.
As I am so noble and beautiful.

You love me so that when I laugh
You are elated to a place above the clouds.
When I blink, you fall into sleep.
When I cry, you drown in a flood of tears.
When I leave, you are the shadow that follows.

But these words do fail, as they slither to me
Like a black snake with its razor tongue.
For we all know love is a game.
But some enjoy it more than others, like those
Who throw the dice with one and move with six.
And I would love you, I truly would,
If you only knew my name, I am no rose.

Humble Surrender

Long grow the leaves
On a surrendering plant,
Long and tender.
A humble surrender it is,
As the leaves shelter the bitter insects
Being trampled by the burly raindrops.
A most humble and noble surrender
To all of God's creation.
Oh, I pray that I may live like a leaf.

Weakness

My soul is weak
I know that now,
As I wipe beads of shame
Off my holy brow.
I gaze up at my Lord
And then at my hoard,
Yet not at the pure and the meek.

Hope Fields

Strolling along rich green fields
On a magnificent sunny day,
I let my happiness roam free.
It seeped into every vein
Giving my body painless electric shocks.
The sun's rays followed me wherever I went,
The welcoming grass bowed down before me.
The humble trees were sorrowful of their great stature
And surrendered themselves to the eager birds,
Humbly and gratefully.
Then my eyes, although lowered
From the sun's penetrating beam,
Saw something unusual;
In the midst of the fields of beauty
Stood a lone tree, dry and sullen.
Struck by a wretched lightening bolt
It accepted its misery,
Completely alone and barren of any green comfort.
It slouched there, ashamed of itself,
Unable to hide its total and utter grief.
My heart pinched for I realised then that;
Somewhere in sorrow lies hope,
Somewhere in hope lies sorrow.

Void

Into the void I hurtle, past the stars and moon.
Is this love? This unending emptiness
Tells me to break loose and fly away soon.
Since it is better to be consumed by nothingness.

Yet a final try, I storm the castle gates ready
To rap my fist upon love's solid door.
I hit my head upon the unyielding oak, unsteady,
I collapse under the blow finding love here no more.

Again empty, again a sieve made from my dreams,
With nobody to whom I may turn.
Love lost eternally, and no friend it seems
Can bring me back from this contemptible yearn.

Perhaps I was wrong to dream, to be ever hopeful
A tale could be real based on imagined delusion.
Now, it seems, I have learnt to be thankful.
I am better equipped to withstand this illusion.

Indifference

Do not imagine I am your slave
Merely because I serve you warmth.
For it is not my love for you
That leads me to your beck and call,
It is another's order that makes me fall.

Do not imagine I am your lover
Merely because I sit while you speak.
For it is not my love for you
That obliges me to hear your song,
Though you need me to shield you from wrong.

Do not imagine I am your friend
Merely because my heart smiling reaches your eyes.
For it is not my love for you
That indulges your fantasies of life,
That listens while you drown in your strife.

Do not imagine I am your saviour
When, drowning, you clasp my loving hand.
For it is not my love for you
That refrains from pulling that tired hand away,
While I stand, noble, like a sculpture of clay.

Do not imagine me so, I am not all I seem,
You expect a raging sea, but I am a stream.
So scream, at the indifference of my state.
And as your tears fall onto the paper
Where you have written your dreams,
Do not imagine the comfort of false hope,
I do not care, and never will it seems.

Blank Screen

A blank screen stares at me, longingly.
But what of the blank screen within me?
I hope nobody can see it.
Because if they do I'm fucked.
I'm hanging onto the remaining parts of myself.
Friends lost in time,
Sweet moments disappearing into oblivion.
Love never there, I hope it comes soon.
But who can love this empty screen,
Which was once so full of hope and dreams?
Now there is only nothing, everything is lost.
No. Not lost. Sold over the years for that pound of flesh.
What price is this?
Of late I have been comforted by this emptiness,
And I pay it gladly.
Now I wander the earth in hateful melancholy
In order to satisfy my sad heart's delusion.
So here I remain, the eternal bohemian, alone.
I pay it. Gladly.

A look inside

I look into myself,
What good can that possibly bring?
Years of insanity sprung from solitude.
A fine bequest indeed!
But what do I see if I stare deeper within?
I see a picture of everyone. Every soul.
But the picture is not mine, anymore.
Any less.

It is this picture within me,
Which tells me who I am.
Who I can be.
Who I must be.
But I cannot see, and never will.
A fine bequest indeed.

Lulu

Lulu stares at the painting on the wall, vivid and raw.
From the swirls of colour a face looks deep into her.
The face of an absurd looking minotaur,
Fashioned from elaborate wispy fur.

A guilty secret lies behind those eyes,
She can feel it crawling up her spine.
As she felt when she stabbed her lover with lies
After their passionate souls would entwine.

Lulu is scared as she sees the colours on
The wall before her. Symbolic writing on the frame
Makes her sing aloud a heartbreaking song,
So she may return to the earth from where she came.

So much guilt she carries like a babe in a sling,
She cannot stop the tsunami in her eyes.
From regret at burying her wedding ring
For earthly gifts and seductive prize.

But no more can she reap the reward of sin
As she is reduced to prowl the street for hasty love.
No more tenderness from the painter; C'est fin!
He hangs with a smile from love's pinnacle above.

And one day a man stops by and requests her
Passion to quench his hidden moral hunger. He rests back
On the bed and from the depths appears that seductive fur
Of the minotaur's colours. She calls to him; "Jack".

So the final throes of regret begin
And Lulu is consumed by the torment of her past.
She has found her soulmate in the pit of sin
And now lies dead on the mattress, free at last.

(based on a story by B. Franklin Wedekind)

Low is Me

That lowly flower bathed in sunlight,
Its beauty masking rotten roots beneath pure soil.
Such is my shame as I scurry in the vulgar night
Quenching my lascivious spirit from which I recoil.

I am the caged lion who weeps
At my base form; so far away from infinity of faculty.
And hatred at my repulsive self seeps
From every pore, for I am low and low is me.

But can I make amends for my basest deeds,
Will Time give me its unconditional love to mend?
Time laughs as he randomly throws down his seeds
And says "Behold, you are near the end"

Here comes the rain

If only the rain would cease!
The patter of drops burst inside my tired brain,
Waking me from trance like slumber.
I take comfort in my current state.
Though, now shell shocked, my slumber has vanished
Into these clear spheres filled with light.
The rain reminds me of past grudges
And now morphs into a river of sadness.
The past does not flow away from me
And rather clings to me like bitter honey.
But the unsullied water falls away from me
And I stand here drenched in madness.
Unable to forget all that was said.
Unable to forget all that was unsaid.
And unable to be cleansed back to purity,
With no way back to the multicoloured arch of light.

Home at Sea

As I sat at ease, watching the playful Sea,
I suddenly began to feel the golden coal
Mercilessly burning into my soft flesh,
And the Sun locking me in its uncompromising glare.
The Sea loudly thrashed against the shimmering diamonds.
I clawed against the golden coal
Trying to find solace in the comforting dim glow,
Cowering from the Sea's temper.
I saw the blue ocean's blackness
As it hurled its beautiful jewels towards the Sun,
In protest at its loveless warmth
That wantonly tore the cold away.
Then, as the Sun drifted away beneath the earth,
I saw the Sea slowly creep towards the terrified shells
To comfort them with his cool calm paternal paws.
And that was when love found its way to me.

Nature

I gaze across the glorious glade and river deep,
No imperfection there I see.
My eyes glisten in mirror of the river's teary seep
As I realise the imperfection lies within me.

The river curves around and flows on and through,
It peaks and troughs in the soil making its way.
Never before did I see birds high above the blue
Circling the world with their elegant sway.

The trees will shelter me from tempestuous force,
Which I sense brewing in the other worlds within.
But though the trees are tall and strong, of course
They cannot protect me from my thoughts of sin.

And that was when I forgot to sing.
The nothingness and emptiness taking control.
No heavy armoury or empowering wing
As I fall, heart first, into this gaping hole.

Nature has left me now, I fall deeper,
I claw at the unearthly well and fall into nothing beneath.
No longer am I my soul's keeper,
My shield fallen away, my sword in its sheath.

And then I land upon the cold hard ground.
A dimly lit ghost of shallow grey,
I carefully try to speak yet there is no sound.
I see myself across the river in the light of day.

My shell sits there, still by the bright blue river.
I stand empty before me, faint in the world of woe.
Suddenly I am holding an old wooden quiver,
So I place the sharp arrow into its ornate bow.

My grey arm pulls back and releases the sharp metal.
The arrow travels straight and true fulfilling its yearn,
Piercing my shell, which scatters into a thousand glass petal,
Disappearing into the ground never to return.

And there my ghost lies in eternal darkness forever.
Alone in nature's perfection, alone in the ether.

Seasons

Winter creeps along far too slowly
With no regard for the warmth of our souls.
Summer hides away in the far corner,
Ashamed of its natural brightness in the face of cold.
Ice melts, rocks erode, everything fades.
Yet nothing fades for the pain lingers there awhile,
Like fossils beneath the shallow earth.
A thin piece of armoury indeed!
It comes away easily beneath my clawed hands
And my heart cries out in agony.

There is no autumn or spring,
Only extremity in the atmosphere.
And like the tempestuous weather I laugh and sing,
Or cry a thousand salty tears which drop on the earth.
And my tears erode the rocks and earth,
And there, exposed, lie the fossils of pain,
So the cycle begins all over again.
Laughter and Song hide behind Summer's glow
And with trepidation they peek into Shadow's cold.
They call out for help, they scream, they yell.
What season is this? I cannot tell.

Maddening Mist

The maddening mist surrounds me
As I walk across the fields of greyish green.
Flanked by prickly shrub and overbearing tree
I gratefully drink this holy winter scene.

It may be that I am in a dream,
It may be that I lie in a coffin cold.
I feel my mind melting into the nearby stream
As I contemplate those I left under the fold.

These burdensome thoughts weigh upon me.
Gripped by a dull sadness from the start,
I was forced to go to the fields to break free
From the indulgent melancholy of my heavy heart.

And now the mist mocks my tears
As it weighs down upon me more and more.
Drops of dew on the blades drown my fears
But then the fear returns as before.

Oh that I could escape this circle of madness
Which engulfs me, stifling my cries.
Though, in truth, if I could I would have much sadness
As I bitterly gaze at the resplendent beauty of the skies.

Earth

Dust settles on barren land.
Particles float above, tauntingly free.
A warm glow emanates from the soft sand
Pining for its brother, the Sea.

But alone is the earth, no nourishment here.
No flowers grow from the dry soil. A colony
Of ants cower in tense fear,
Their bodies will disintegrate but their souls will be.

A fleeting recollection of memories past,
Of greens and blues and love.
Instead a thundering vibration wakes us at last
And brings us back. But we recoil as we look above.

The end of the world has come to us now.
A momentary panic gives way, in authority we trust.
We look at ourselves in disbelief thinking how
Could we not save us from dust to ashes, ashes to dust.

Air

A paper bag sits on the pavement, aloof and still.
Empty, waiting for love to come.
And then a stirring from behind the hollow hill,
As the wind finds its way there from behind the sun.

A gush of force flies through
The street causing the wicked much distress.
Yet it brought no wrath and transparently flew,
Kissing the bag with its sweet caress.

And so the refreshing breeze waltzes
In and out of the still air.
Gently weaving its secrets into the recesses,
Leaving clues towards its heavenly lair.

The wind swirls rhythmically in melodious dance.
The bag spins around in ecstasy
Like a dreidal, spinning into a frenzied trance,
And then rocking to its sides like a solemn tree.

No gust, no hurricane, no dramatic metaphor,
Just the simplicity of breath across this blessed place.
The secrets in the wind shall be for evermore
Etched within the timelessness of majestic space.

Water

Frozen rock erodes under the gentle wave,
Which paws at its icy shell. Minerals dissolve
Into fizzing water. It is now too late to save
The world from the boiling pits to which we devolve.

Blue cool lake before us, we drink in its tranquillity.
Blue cool sky above us, protecting us from glare,
Though not quite. Yellow rays penetrate the deepening sea
And all the while we sit on the shore edge and stare.

Moist mist engulfs us as we look towards the lake,
Oblivious to the reasons for the impending flood.
We begin our downfall and will now forsake
Nature, to drown in our forefathers' blood.

More than love, more than emotion flowing through our soul,
The sad truth oozes out and settles on the dew.
A drop from above causes the sea to divide in two
As foretold before and again until the desert fills the hole.

Fire

Dancing flames, they sway before me like dervishes,
Seducing me with their jagged lights.
A hollow regret is heard through the excesses
As they shine, like a geisha in a rich man's sights.

And as the regret is scorched into oblivion
A sigh of relief penetrates the skies.
But, alas, regret cannot disappear from passionate action
And instead, phoenix like, it will again rise.

And so uncontrolled and flamboyant the heat moves on,
The flames proceed to destroy everything in sight.
So as we look upon the charred remains of life all gone
It is easier to remember the burn and forget the light.

By the River

Sitting silently by the woods, my beloved beside me,
I touch the gentle grass with my fingers and toes.
I look deep into the sun's mirror; the son of the Sea,
To discover myself, for he knows
Every inch of my reflection. He sees
Every atom of my flawed being.
So I stretch my legs, rest my head against the trees,
Hoping perchance to dream in waking.
A wave of euphoric mist drifts towards me
And envelops us while we sit in meditative ecstasy.

But then I awake asking the world about my soul,
Waiting for an answer in the moist breeze. I wait forever,
And yet, there is no answer to fill this gaping hole.
I wait some more and fashion a crown from sprigs of heather
And I watch a swallow gliding free through the blue above,
I see its peaceful state, its acceptance of the present.
It spins through the skies like a dervish in love.
Yet my obsessive intellect must know from where I was sent.
And I wait on the warm earth and drink the moist drops of air
While my beloved consumes mother nature with his soul laid bare.

Many years pass sitting by the river bank in quiet meditation
And now we are old and grey. I see the same swallow
Gliding playfully over the water in elation
And yet my answer has not come and I feel hollow.
I see my beloved melt into the grass, the trees, the water
Where he happily floats away towards the sea.
A smile spreads through my being as I have my answer;
For I am him and he is me.

Road to Salvation

The road to salvation is paved with thorns.
I walked that road carrying a basket full of Guilt on my shoulders.
I admired my reflection in the river that ran beside me;
A prophetic image of bleeding feet and water filled eyes.
I walked for an eternity
Before I finally arrived at the gates of gold and pearl.
But they were closed to me.
I rapped my fist against the gates
But there was no answer.
I beat my head against the gates
And my crown of thorns pierced into my skull.
"Why?" shouted I, "Why may I not enter, for all my suffering and torment?
Why have you forsaken me my rightful place at the throne of salvation?"
And the answer came thus and shook me to my very core;
"Salvation sits not on a throne, but on the cold hard earth.
And though you arrive here with your lofty belief in your path,
Your path is wrong and you must go back.
Salvation does not come from arrogant self sacrifice,
Indulgent guilt, or bargainable forbearance with those who have wronged you.
It comes with no contrived ideas of right and wrong.
There is no path to salvation. You must simply live,
And when you do, live in the moment,
From moment to moment.
Salvation will then seep into your soul
And you will not even notice it.
It exists within you and only needs to be begotten over time.
And you have time.
Go back my child, salvation lies within you."
I listened with tears streaming down my face
And sunk into the cold hard earth.
And that was when I realised, I would go to the fire.

Journey

My source of life beats in time to my footsteps
On the cobbled path to Truth.
I feel it within me, singing with angelic melody.
A beautiful symphony touches my soul and I am thankful.
I walk on with my guide beside me.
He holds my hand protectively and smiles at me.
"Where am I walking" I ask. No sound comes,
Just the music which keeps playing,
Faintly when I am doubtful,
Loudly when I can feel my heart beat in my chest.
I am listening in now, mesmerised
By colours emanating from the sound.
Greens, reds, blues and a flash of white light forces its way through.
The colours break into a thousand pieces,
Like glass, and they fall away leaving only white.

I am floating now,
I look around and realise that I have reached a chapel.
My guide has disappeared into the light,
Or I have disappeared into the darkness,
I cannot tell and I feel infinitely alone.

I am now in the desert.
Tears are flowing from my eyes as I look around
At a vast expanse of sand,
Feeling vulnerable to the elements.
I deeply miss my past life which, although fraught with regret,
Was far away from solitude.
And lo, I see a face before me, so pure I cannot comprehend its detail.
It is a woman, covered in a long black cloak,
Holding a baby and looking at me with gentle eyes full of love.
Is this a mirage?
I cannot tell, but I am at once at peace.

It is Mother Mary.
She greets me in a melodic voice and tells me to look for His signs.
If I see them, she says, I will have found what I am looking for.
I look away, puzzled, but when I look back she is gone.
I again feel the weight of solitude upon my tired shoulders
And I collapse onto the ground. I dig my fingers into the warm sand,
I look up at the ocean blue sky and overpowering yellow rays of the sun.
I am slowly soothed by the warmth around me, and then,
As I stare at the beauty surrounding me, I can see His signs everywhere.
Stretching back on the sand I look up, smiling,
Content that I have found my Lord.

Loveless soul

How can I know how to love,
The warped compass that I am?
The cogs are running through my brain;
A calculating realist, prepared to survive
In this unnatural world.

How can I know how to feel
Within the nostalgic idea of human nature?
I search for a guide, an instruction book,
Anything, to tell me of my heart.
It was here inside me, a long long time ago.
And yet now there is nothing of feeling.
Only fine food, money, and a clock;
One to sustain my functioning earthly vehicle.
One to help me in this false world.
And one to tell me I am of no consequence.

So as shards of time fall before my path
I know that I will be here no more.
A blankness unlike anything I have ever known
Envelops my very existence,
Until I am lost in the mist,
Unable to find my way back.
My last breath whispers out into the heavy air;
"Here lies the legacy of this mechanical being,
A soul unable to love".

Entertain me with the Battlefield

He loved entertaining
But cried when he saw my Nazi sign.
Couldn't hold the love that was fading,
He kept a sun that could not shine.
If God was a villain, he'd be me,
The world would burn in fire.
Contemplating commandments, parting the sea,
We'd be spinning in a hopeless gyre.

If you were with me I would smile,
With warmth would I settle.
Instead I can only smell a vile
Stench of rotting petal.

If I put the stars on your feet
Could you not go forth to the battlefield.
If, by pen, freedom you could meet
Could you not trample over the promising yield.
If, however, you have to go,
I cannot say that I love you, so
Fight me without my protective shield,
Please entertain me with the battlefield.

Not in my name

I hear Ibrahim's voice over the barrage;
"Am I an animal? I often wonder.
I have the look of a human being.
You would not believe it
But I look just like you!
And yet, I am an animal.
Or maybe a thing. Some thing,
Used by either side of these cold walls,
Which constrict my ever lowly existence.
I can see my friend looking down at me.
I look deep into his eyes;
I think he can see glimmers of humanity in me.
I think.
His father is teaching me a lesson
For all the wrong that has spilled out from my land.
But it is not my land, not now. I am an animal,
With no home to speak of.
And yet, I see my friend in pain.
I want to scream; not in my name!
But he cannot hear my cries,
I think he must hate me now.

But here I cower, surrounded by hate, trapped by fear.
A silent scream, an unseen tear.
And so now I will die.
My life worthless, my death ignored.
A meaningless existence am I"

I hear Abraham's voice over the flares:
"I see my friend with tears of fear
As my father beats him repeatedly.
I shout at my father to stop,
I would throw myself down and ask him to beat me.
But my father, who I love and trust,

Tells me he has done great evil in our land.
But how could my friend do evil?
He is small and meek.
I pity him, but I should not, my father says.
My father, who I love and trust,
Tells me a lesson must be learnt
And he will teach it.
And yet, I see my friend in pain.
I want to scream; not in my name!
But he cannot hear my cries,
I think he must hate me now."

I have sinned against my mother

I have sinned against my mother
For I have walked away into the night.
A deep hunger within my soul
For some substance to this wretched life.
I have left her cradling an empty space.
My temperament inherited from a raging storm,
My eyes filled with sand dunes of distant land.
And there she sits on the bed where I was born
While my wings continue to flap in desperation;
"Away, fly away" my demon calls to me,
And as I climb higher I see her lonely figure
And I pray that I may die in the cool pure air.
I have betrayed the heart of my mother
For I have walked away into the darkness.

I have sinned against my father

I have sinned against my father
For I have ignored his calls to me.
I have looked away at the bustling crowd
Hoping that they would look back at me.
But they turn away, repelled by my hungry eyes.
They laugh and joke and sing.
And I laugh, I joke, I sing, with hollow breaths,
The great mimic that I am.
I have left him holding a hollow shell.
My desolation, gifted to me when I was born,
Is now a towering force in his house. I run,
Into the crowd, the song of the alien now faint in the mob.
I have betrayed the heart of my father
For I have walked away into the darkness.

The Devil hath no song

The Devil hath no song
Yet he dances through our hearts and mind.
The river of fear is deep and long
As it meanders through our thoughts unkind.

That tempting lute plays on
In my mind's tired ear. It's all
I can do to save my soul. Play on!
And I will take that glorious fall.

And now I sail
Towards heartbreak and timelessness.
I navigate only to fail,
And drown in the tide of my success.

And yet there is that shimmer,
That beacon of hope, that glimmer!
And the music guides me to repentance.

Night and Day

How does the Day cope with being apart
From its natural love, the Night?
Their painful separation from the start
Could pierce the hearts of angels bright.

Their respective duties for our benefit
Have hidden sweet longing for the half of the pair.
If only this sacrifice was made clear, just a little bit,
They would have had a choice, but what choice is there?

No darkness or no light; What would become of us between?
Day laughs, Night cries a thousand tears into a stream.

The longing more painful now without hope or choice,
The pain now more intense in their prison alone.
And yet, in their hearts is a singing voice
Telling them they are blessed, for they are one.

The Slanted House

A slanted house sits atop a mountain.
Its mottled clay bricks showing signs of its age,
Like the slanting tree beside it. A lonely figure,
It stoops there with no emerald soul displayed,
It stands empty, always slanting back to its only friend.
The foundations and roots of the house and tree
Cling onto the mountain's welcoming earth.
Their claws grasping steadfast whilst the wind tries to
Topple them over and down the mountain's elegant back
Into the village below. Villagers look up expecting the fall,
But the perverse sadness consuming the house and tree
Will not let them fall and will prolong their solitude.
So, it seems, their natural instinct for self preservation
Keeps them holding on. "But", ponder the villagers,
"Surely the instinct is eroding now into the nearby stream?
They will both fall as they cannot survive up there alone!"
The mountain lets out a loud rumbling laugh,
Which reverberates through the hearts of the villagers.
"Look atop my head" says the mountain,
"You see a house and tree slanting towards each other;
A powerful display of all conquering love!
They live quietly content in each other's presence
Holding on for love, not self preservation.
They are fearful, not of falling but of leaving the other.
So fear not my people, marvel at my house and tree,
For with this slanting love I am crowned in glory"

Mariachi

The sound of the Mariachi whispers softly
Within the hollow depths of my mind.
An echo.
The gentle singing reminds me of a smile.

A Boy

A boy sits on the wall,
His eyes betray infinite suns and stars.
A parable, a verse, so pure and tall.
A message from God or tree or Mars?

A boy looks down at us below
As we fight and tussle and scream.
He has no voice and cannot show
Us our world is nothing more than a dream.

A boy waits for eternity.
Searching through our collective heart and mind
For signs of hope and divinity,
Before we are lost and left behind.

A boy looks up towards the skies,
He knows the futility of his selfless love.
So he stands, spreads his wings and flies
To his heavenly sanctuary above.

In the Cave

In the cave my thoughts float and dance,
I sing in remembrance of my truth.
I walk through utopia and reach a peaceful trance,
While my angel plays his magical flute.

If anyone could see me now they would surely smile
At my arrogant belief in higher light.
And yet I will stay here for a while
As heavenly gifts are within my sight.

I see the mountain before me tall and proud,
I see an abundance of His signs before me.
So I look into my soul and reach for my cloak to enshroud
My heart in its warmth and dignity.

And now I reach peace, slowly
I tread with trepidation into the unknown.
The light illuminates my soul and body
And I am transported to my home.

Fatimah

Fatimah sits under a tall imposing date palm tree
And looks up at the expanse of sky above.
How small she feels in her ragged attire.
She examines the blisters on her hands and feet
And rough worn skin on her weary shoulders.
She can make out the jagged lines of water pails.
Her hands touch her hollow cheeks,
Eroded through a steady stream of tears
For her father, mother, husband and sons,
And for all her kin of past, present and future.

Fatimah digs her feet into the sand,
And rests her aching back on the protective bark of the tree.
The love for her father and nature is all she needs
To nourish her soul. She sees a passing Trader
Riding his camel to the marketplace.
He looks at her with subtle arrogance,
How like a beggar she looks, so small and insignificant.
He allows his camel to kick sand at her and laughs
As he drops coins onto the floor near her hands.
Such a small inconsequential stooped figure she is,
Yet he is much deceived.
For beneath that fractured shell is a secret.
A warm glow hides below, ready to illuminate the world,
When the time comes.

Fatimah is still, her armour is evaporating
Like a mist clearing from the path of the sun.
Her husband's shield is gone
Yet she is protected by the elements.
A faint smile spreads onto her cracked lips
For she is returning to her father, her beloved,
And her Lord.

Fatimah az Zahra is seated on her throne,
Her dearest Mother beside her.
The Trader is brought before them and he looks
At the scales, a feather and heart before him.
His heavy heart drops and he lets out a cry
As his past sins shoot regret into his soul like lightning.
Then his Lord's voice pulsates through the atmosphere,
The Trader has been condemned yet forgiven.

Fatimah is given her reward for all her suffering,
She is now mistress at the day of judgment.
"My reward" she says "Is to be here,
Beside my parents, beside my Lord"
"And what of me?" asks the Trader.
Says Fatimah; "You gave me coins to feed my body
And sand to feed my soul. To you I am thankful"
The Trader's eyes fill with tears
As he looks up at her majestic beauty.
He thinks of his brothers.
"And what of your children", he asks.
Fatimah looks deep at him
With sadness and unconditional light.
She says simply, "I do not know".

The Return

Is it the clouds that drift away,
Or I? Or my drifting thoughts?
Does the darkness therein engulf my soul,
Or the darkness within me.
For there is no darkness without me.

Perhaps I should run into the sky,
And face myself and my reality.
But I am happier to sink into the ground
Devouring others' purity.
And I am happier still to sink further
Till the clouds are but a distant memory,
And I am content in the blackness of my heart.
And here I shall remain within the earth that made me.
Be joyful, for I have returned.

The Silver Moon

And so we gaze towards the heavenly starlight;
Those lofty heights to which we aspire.
Secretly wishing to take flight
Above these lowly depths of the mire.

We pray for a strong walled sanctuary
To protect us from the world's wickedness.
We pray for the armour of luminosity
And a blade of emotive fierceness.

Look, my child, at the silver moon,
Melt in those pure beams of white.
Be ready, for you will fly away soon,
So let yourself disappear into the light.

Edge of the World

A tumult of laughter echoes in the Thinker's mind.
He sits on the edge of the world trying to ignore
The babbling rabble, the folk unkind.
The tumult gets louder, the crowds sneer some more.

The Thinker smiles at the laughter
For that seems the obvious choice.
Better laugh than cry, thinks the Thinker,
And he opts for the more rational voice.

The Feeler comes to join him by the world's frame,
Tears running down her face, head drooping low.
Thinker tells Feeler to ignore the world's sad game
For they are not mindful of their words, they do not know.

At this the Feeler lets out a howl of laughter
And regards the Thinker with bright eyes of the Sea.
"Once you step into the world, dear brother,
Then you may explain its ways to me."

Paper Lion

A paper Lion sits by my tree.
No sign of life, it sits quiet and still.
It guards the fragile soul of me;
My beautiful farm and quaint grey mill.

This structure a monument of my life's labour,
The indents in the walls are signs of my years.
It is returning to this emblem that I love and savour,
To be apart from its shelter is the sum of my fears.

The lion moves gently in the cool breeze,
No roar but a rustling of leaves and wood.
Its eyes stare ahead and there it sees
Those Strangers, and would attack if it could.

They bound over the hill towards my home,
No remorse as they infringe on my rightful spaces.
So I sit here in my sanctuary, angry and alone,
Staring at their foreign faces.

They reach my home with tired eyes
And tell of their land lost in the tumult of hate.
A burden so great it reaches the skies,
Their earthly souls now vanished in the hands of fate.

They gather around my mill, sit by the fire,
Drink and sing songs of hope tinged with sadness.
Their troubles evaporate on love's forgiving pyre,
And a tear drops from my eyes, I gladly confess.

I step out of my mill and join them on the ground,
We merrily sing together until the end of time.
The Lion protects us all as we sing of love found,
My soul no longer of bricks and our hearts entwine.

Memory

Maybe I was not there when my world began,
Yet I see the sepia memories before me.
These moments in time did exist I understand,
And yet, I have no memory.

I carefully turn the pages of the album with a sad smile,
I run my creased fingers over the flawless faces.
Was I in those moments or asleep all the while,
Or did I exist between the moments in the empty spaces.

What do I remember, asks my confused head,
As I turn the few pages which exist in my mind.
I remember my children who bring food to my sickbed
But then I forget them when they leave me behind.

And what of me? Why can I not recall
My past incarnation now drowned in a forgotten pool.
If I have no memory did I really exist at all?
Or did my world begin as this sad old fool.

Grey Ghosts

The carriage hurtles along the beaten track,
A cold metal coffin, yet full of life it speeds on.
In it a thousand grey ghosts.
Each in their own carriage of glass,
Each consumed by a thought, or a word,
Or notes of music dancing above their heads.
Full of life they are, yet somehow comatose.
Numb to the extremities of the world outside.
They meander through reflection as the carriage dashes on.
And what hurtles between the corners of their minds?
What thoughts resonate past the bright yellow and white
Collage of information,
And faces in secret meditation?
I cannot tell, a mystery lies before me.
Yet this grey ghost dreams of lands beyond,
Of family loved and friends to come.
Of adventure sought, like those of heroes gone.
And yet at other times of friends lost,
Or time passing by with the speed of the carriage.
Adventure missed, and monotony marked
By the gleaming arrow of Fortune,
Who has decided these course of events,
Which we pass through with no impact.
Yes, much like this carriage we are,
Passing through life, passing always.

Shadows

Once upon a time, before time began,
There lay a child on earth's hallowed green.
It rested there awhile, bathed in sunlight,
Naked and pure. Still in the gentle breeze.
Eyes closed to the world, closed to the ugly truth.

When its eyes opened the shadows slowly crept from afar
Towards the babe, with black claws reaching over him.
The babe opened them some more
And the shadows crawled up his body,
Reaching his eyes where the shadows gathered
And entered there, leaving a trace
Of their black mark beneath his once innocent eyes.

The babe let out a heart wrenching cry,
Now exposed to the world, to the pain.
The shadows permanently etched in his mind,
Now inextricably linked to his once pure soul.

The screams swept through the world
Somewhere between sleeping and waking.
And all heard the babe's cries
Pierce through their dreams.
And then.

And then the man awoke to the deafening scream
But took heart that it was just a dream.
He went to the mirror and saw the mark
Of shadows cometh from the world of dark.

And then the snow melted

And then the snow melted
To reveal the hideous truth beneath.
Effigies of monotony stand cowering,
Now naked before our opening eyes.
Nature's cruel torment is stark
And we recoil back into our concrete shells,
Unable to stand what we have created,
We pray for purifying specks of white.

But it never comes.
Instead it gives birth to folklore
As we exaggerate its beauty and cry at the sun.
Those unremorseful penetrating beams
Rip our concrete shells open
And we lie there trembling on the ground;
Unable to cope with the bad,
Unable to cope with the good,
Unable to withstand nature's monstrous power.

And then an eternity has passed.
We have rebuilt the earth in our image;
Weak and beautiful, powerful and ugly.
A laughable failure once again.
And we stare at our creation,
Praying for a second chance
To undo all our wrongs.
We look upwards, blinkingly, expectantly,
A lonely tear slides down our cheek.
And then the glorious redemption comes
Like pieces of heaven falling on the cold earth.
This unexpected result is now before us
Of hope blossoming from bitter salt.

Ithaca

Oh that I could fly over the scenic blue,
High above these curtailing sails of white!
I would reach my destination; My Ithys, my True!
And freely fall, spinning, like an enchanted kite.
And here, as I sail closer to my goal
Contentment spreads through my soul,
For I am returned to my home.

My old bones creaking like my aged ship
That has travelled with me through worlds afar.
And yet, I feel youthful euphoria and my worries slip,
I sail on, navigated by that auspicious star.
And here, reaching this sacred land,
I joyfully run my fingers through the warm sand,
For I am returned to my home.

Oh that I could live forever in my Ithaca, my home.
That I could remain within its bosom in contented bliss.
So I fashion an ethereal blade from my companion tome
And bless the earth with my pious kiss.
And here, enveloped like a model of clay, I sink in ecstasy,
In devout worship of the land that made me,
For I am returned to my home.

II.
TALES

Fallen

Particles float around my aching head. Specks of light dance around me like fairies. Where did I put my Soul? I look around, blinkingly, trying to recover from the blow to my head. I try to find my guardian angel but all I can see is a gun on the floor. What was the point of that? What was the point of any of it, I ask my, still aching, Brian. He doesn't know.

I steady myself and then try to get up. If I start moving maybe I'll be able to figure it all out. Brian tells me "We have been asked to remain at this platform until this matter is resolved". Goddamn jobsworth! Brian tells me to be quiet and shows me a girl walking down the street. Her bob cut hair bouncing in time with each step, headphones glued to her pixie ears, and her eyes focused on the pavement laid out before her. Oh now I remember! I used to sing to her. Many years ago before she was born. When she was nothing more than a miniature human doll in her mother's womb. A body no bigger than a peanut and a soul as large as an elephant, for she is part of me and my soul is huge. If only I could find it.

A lifetime has gone by with me still on the floor. I look up and see that I am facing an altar in a dimly lit church. I see that famous tortured body, bloodied and stretched before me, yet I cannot fathom how anyone could feel as much pain as I do right now. Those deep blue eyes stare into me and let my arrogant self know that I know nothing of pain. Brian agrees with the eyes. I try to balance myself and move on to my knees. The gesture looks like perfect penance considering I'm in a church. Now where was I? Oh yes, I remember, the peanut who grew into a beautiful woman, who almost got me killed. But, I casually say to Brian, one shouldn't let a thing like that cloud one's judgment. Brian ignores me and looks around for the girl; the last piece of the jigsaw, the emblem of my forgotten life.

It all started, as most good stories do I suppose, in a pub called the Pig & Whistle. The owner, a curmudgeonly sort of fellow, was preparing for a lock-in and the regulars were gulping down their brews and staring down the pretentious college kids who were finishing their drinking games. I was a young barman; intelligent, fairly handsome and athletic, all ticks on every girl's list except that I wasn't rich. I worked in the bar on weeknights and in a café opposite a secondary school on weekdays. These two jobs were barely enough to cover my rent in my apartment in Angel. The thing is that I was particularly religious and brought up as a good Christian boy in my home town of Los Angeles. So when I moved to London at the age of 22 to follow my dream of becoming a writer, I couldn't imagine living anywhere else. I had decided that London was sufficiently bohemian for me and so I left behind the watchful eyes of the City of Angels to the guardianship of a single Angel, and it proved to be a defining point in my life, as you will soon see.

I realise that I have strayed a little so I will get back to my story, but Brian has assured me that these details will fall into place once we get onto the jigsaw girl. After I had diligently scrubbed the tables, cleared the glasses, and sneakily swigged any leftover beer, I started to get ready to leave for home. I gathered my manuscript that I had been working on in my breaks and walked towards the front of the bar. And that was when I saw the most beautiful pirate in the world! Now I will admit that I had never come across a pirate before so I had no legitimate point of comparison, however, the woman who stood in front of me was exquisitely beautiful. Her hair and clothes were dripping wet as if she had just escaped the wreckage of her drowning ship. She wore a cutlass on her belt and baggy pants which, whilst wet, seemed to cling to the definition of her legs. Her pirate hat was askew and sodden tufts of jet black curly hair sprung out from underneath, giving her face the perfect frame. And what a face! Deep black unnerving eyes looking in my direction, sharp cheekbones and a half smile naturally sitting on her full lips. I was so caught up in staring at her I didn't realise that I was, well, staring at her. She shifted uncomfortably at first at this slack jawed barman making an idiot of himself and then made light of the situation by saying "In case you're wondering, I haven't jumped ship". This resulted in nervous laughter from the inebriated Neanderthal collective, so she continued "I was lost in the rain trying to find my way to a fancy dress party, so I thought I'd come inside and regroup for a moment if that's ok?". The bar owner grunted something as he fiddled with the radiator, which seemed to be consent because she nervously sat down at a table nearest the door.

Brian laughs when he tells me what I did next. I strolled over to the pirate with as much nonchalance as I could muster, which incidentally was zero, and tried to say hello. Unfortunately, as I did no sound exited my lips and the pirate stared at me, probably wondering what this odd looking mime artist wanted from her and naturally assuming that I was a deranged drug dealer trying to peddle amphetamines to an innocent girl who just wanted to get out of the rain.

"Hi" she suddenly said, saving me from further embarrassment, "My name's Mandy", and with that I was reborn. I stammered back my name and with my returning confidence I told her that I was a writer and she immediately looked impressed. Since she picked up my American drawl I told her I was originally from Los Angeles, and I could sense that also impressed her. I talked at length about what I was doing in London and my dreams and aspirations until eventually Brian told me to calm down and stop chattering like an idiot about my entire life story, since there wasn't really much to tell, but it was difficult to stop talking when those eyes were looking directly into me. I seriously felt that I could confess all my secrets to her then and there. I chivalrously, but actually selfishly, offered to take Mandy back to her bed and breakfast since I knew where it was. Even if I didn't I would have said I knew anyway and simply walked her home for eternity.

The next thing I remember was an explosion. Walking with Mandy in the cool night air I felt the urge to make sure the bar was where I left it. I looked back, NEVER look back, nothing good ever comes from looking back. I saw that the bar had combusted into tiny fragments and malevolent strobes of light were blinding passers by. A nebulous blanket of panic filled the surrounding air and mixed in with the dark clouds of smoke. Gone! In an instant, my life, gone.

I carried on walking, not caring whether Mandy ran after me or not. She was bad news, Brian told me, she has the mark of bad luck on her. But what did any of it matter anymore? All I knew is that I had to get back to my house, to my angel. Mandy followed me. She followed me for two years! And as much as I loved her, as much as I could feel myself continually enveloped in her beauty, I could not forget the initial horrifying flames that began the start of our relationship.

Then one wintry day in January I was seated in my living room surrounded by a cornucopia of my literary investments when I heard Mandy walk in through the front door, quiet as a fox. She walked into the living room and studied me, sitting on the floor, pencil inclined and ready to write if only my inspiration would come.

"I'm going to name it Ludwig if it's a boy" I looked up and stared at her with a horrified look on my face. Mandy scowled at me and scrunched her nose, which I always found adorable, and continued "And I'm going to name it Valerie if it's a girl". Val, the name formed on my lips. It fit perfectly for my daughter. My daughter! Even now it feels strange saying it.

The pregnancy was quiet and unassuming, just typical of Mandy. I was writing my masterpiece and had no time to be there. And when I say 'there' I mean the earth; the here and now of day to day existence. A pretentious creature I am I know but aren't all us authors of the same ilk?

The day preceding Val's birth was probably the most productive and creative of my life. I remember being up all night, then all day, then all night again. But when you're at your creative best time just falls away. My eyes were bloodshot but glowing with an almost super human energy. My body was too tired to keep up but my mind would not listen to its cries and simply carried on playing its literary symphony. Letters were spinning around my head until they reached their destined place on the page, not to be hurried. And there; my work was finished at last.

I will not tell you the name of the book I completed that sunny morning in July, since if I do you will almost certainly know the name of this author, but it suffices to say that it was a best seller in the UK. My only regret is that whilst I have had considerable success with my later novels, this particular one remained my best.

I remember running my fingers over the pages I had just completed with tears stinging my eyes. My very being spilling out onto cheap sheets of A4 notepaper. And then the loud and impatient phone rang, waking me from my trance like state. Since I had fallen in love with Mandy I could see that a series of unfortunate events were going to unfold before me but I could scarcely bring myself to believe it at first. As I made my way to the hospital I felt an ominous foreboding but could not quite place why I felt that way. Is it possible that I had time travelled beforehand and was now experiencing some feeling of déjà vu? Or had I developed abilities of clairvoyance? I could not tell. I walked and walked towards the hospital expecting the worst to happen.

I knew it as I got to the hospital. I could tell from their faces what they were going to tell me. Mandy had vanished, vaporised into oblivion, leaving an empty sleeve of her body and a crying child. I didn't think death in childbirth happened in western countries anymore. Maybe I had caused it somehow? No, I put that thought out of my mind as quickly as it came. And so, the angel I had fallen in love with, if I was ever capable of such a thing, had turned from a metaphorical angel into a very real one. They told me I had a daughter waiting for me but I didn't even register her. I didn't look at her, I just turned and walked away. No, ran away. Away from the shouts of admonishment from the nursing staff. They don't know the half of it, I thought. I ran all the way back home, not London home, I ran all the way to the City of Angels to drown in the tears of my own making.

One morning many years later I was making myself some coffee in my plush Los Angeles home. I studied my kingdom before me, built up over the years from the success of my first book. Man, I am one lucky bastard! I actually got rich doing the thing I love to do. As I sat down on my porch with my steaming mug of coffee and a newspaper before me, a memory suddenly hit me, so suddenly that it almost knocked my drink over.

I was sat in Hyde Park with Mandy, gazing up at the chill blue London sky, utterly at peace. She stared at me with those mesmerizing eyes whilst I pretended not to notice her. After a while she reached into her jacket pocket and took out a gold locket. It was oval shaped with embossed gold patterns on the front. I opened it and there was a picture of Mandy, looking astonishingly beautiful.

"I want you to have it", she said as her fingers fondled the chain, somehow not wishing to let go of it. I noticed that there was no place for another picture and as I turned the pendant over in my hands I could sense Mandy's penetrating gaze upon me.

"They didn't have a double picture locket, so that's why it's a sole". A wide smile broke on her face in recognition of what she had just said. "I thought you could do with one, a sole that is". The name stuck and my locket became my 'Soul', and although I had hoped Mandy had been joking that I did not have a soul before I met her, I think she had a point.

It's funny how random memories stop you in your tracks and then link onto some remnant of your past that's crying out to you, for whatever reason. One of those mysterious connections to the soul I guess. Like that shop you *always* pass on your way to the train station that's *always* closed but that you are convinced holds some secret to your self. So anyway, that's what made me think of Val, a piece of jewellery, a piece of her mother. And then the interlocking chain began to appear before me, and when I looked between each connecting link I rather thought I could see the faces of all the people who had left me. "No" says Brian, "you mean all the people you left behind". I tried to ignore this and continued to sip my coffee, now ready to start the day.

The phone was ringing, loud and urgent. I dragged my zombified body from my bed to the phone and killed the ever annoying phone ring in one fell swoop. The fastest half asleep phone slinger in the west! It was my girlfriend, Tracey, on her way home from her night shift where she was stock taking at the local convenience store. I think she was asking me for a ride but I couldn't be sure because at that moment I could see an envelope on the table next to the phone, addressed to me in spidery handwriting. There was no post mark so it must have been hand delivered. I picked up the envelope, all the while with Tracey's nervous chattering in my ear, and peered inside. There was a single sheet of paper with the words "Griffith park, tomorrow, at noon". There was no indication of who it could possibly have been from. I put the receiver down, forgetting that Tracey was still on the line. I lay back on my bed and stared up at my dull white ceiling, thoughts whirring through my mind like flies in a glass box. "Who could it be?" I thought, the flood gates of curiosity had opened and there was no way of closing them, at least not for me. I lay there for a while imagining all kinds of possibilities; a stalker, a kidnapper, an ocean's eleven style heist, a movie producer, no, I think the ocean's eleven style heist would be the more probable eventuality. The thoughts continued to run through my head like a film reel until one final thought came winging its way to me; "Boy, Tracey's gonna be pissed when she gets in!"

The next morning, brimming with excitement and intrigue, I stood in Griffith park at the place specified on a map contained with the note. I had on a pair of jeans however I had forgotten how uncomfortable they were and I nervously kept shifting my weight in them to lessen the chaffing against my legs. One hand resting against the lonely tree and the other hand in my pocket anxiously turning over a quarter between my fingers. "Maybe I should walk away" I thought, "Maybe I should just leave ... right now! This is so fucking stupid", and then, in the corner of my eye appeared a person standing in the distance. An ominous figure waiting by a tree, looking directly at me. It was a woman and I immediately felt relieved without quite knowing why. She suddenly began to walk in my direction. "She's going to kill you" Brian was yelling in my ear, "She's going to bury you right here in Griffith park and your grave will be nothing more than a place for skater boys and urinating dogs, is that what you want?". I blinked my eyes a couple of times and could make out the woman more clearly, she was old with a weathered face and penetrating eyes. She had a permanently serious frown as if she was about to give me a good telling off. She carried on walking towards me and then reached into her coat, "Oh shit!" screamed Brian, "She's got a gun, get the hell out of here!" I instinctively raised my heels slightly, ready to sprint away, when I realised that the gun she had just taken out of her coat looked remarkably like an envelope and nothing at all like a gun.

"You are [my name]" she said, in a distinctly Russian accent.

"Yes I am [my name]" I hesitantly replied.

"Here" she pushed the envelope into my chest, rather forcefully I might add. "You take this!". I reached my hand up to my chest and prised the envelope shaped gun from her bony fingers. And with that she turned right around and walked back in the direction she had come. I stood there, empty and confused.

I sat down in a quiet local cafe and ordered a coffee. I took in the bleak décor around me and felt a familiar sense of foreboding. I had an irrational fear that the café would blow into smithereens and nobody would even notice. People would walk by, and the remains of the café beneath which we were all buried would go completely unnoticed, despite the screams from the shuddering rubble.

Then the waitress woke me from my daze and placed the aromatic coffee in front of me. I took a sip, burning my mouth, and then I remembered the envelope. I slowly opened it and looked at the spidery handwriting with disbelieving eyes:

"You are a wretched coward. You ruined my daughter's life and you abandoned my granddaughter whom I have raised into a beautiful young woman. Now, she needs a father, she needs to know where she is from. It may please you to hear that I am now nearing the last few breaths of my life and I simply want Val to know who you are and that you're still around. Even though you … [*pages of slanderous insinuation and conjecture from a bitter old woman, that is not relevant to the story and that we don't really need to go into*] … She is in London at the moment, here is her address"

A faint smile spread across my face at this point. Although I was, shall we say, indifferent to my mother-in-law's impending death, the reason I was smiling was because Val had decided to live in Angel. "That's my girl!" I thought, and then was surprised at myself because she hadn't been my girl for 18 years. I sipped the now lukewarm coffee and let it melt into my tongue. I felt guilt take over my body but I let it happen, completely willingly. I would enjoy this feeling just as it was, since I had already decided to make amends. Sweet guilt, I think they call it.

London was very different to the last time I was here. The roads were much safer, I thought, as I dodged the cars in the West End. I found myself next to the horses statue in Leicester Square, looking around at the throngs of people around me. I slipped into the Trocadero and brought myself a tea (when in Rome!) and a muffin (sometimes Rome needs a muffin), and stood beside a shop wall watching the tourists ambling around me. I realised then that I was simply trying to delay the inevitable and, grudgingly but determined to do my duty, I set out again into the ridiculously busy streets. Tourists were now stepping over each other and staring open mouthed at the surroundings. They looked as if they wanted to ask directions from one of the unfriendly passers by, yet ignored me, despite my very obvious eye contact. I wanted to shake them by the scruffs of their necks and beat them about the head with their inappropriately expensive digital cameras and shout "Don't you know you I am? I used to live here!" But I didn't and I realise now that making eye contact in London is a sure fire sign that you're either crazy or not from London, so I suppose the Tourists had the right idea somewhat.

I found myself in the tube station, floating down the escalators as if in a bizarre dream. I blankly got on the tube carriage of the Northern Line in order to take the long way round to Angel. I glanced at the line map on the carriage and then, astonished, blinked a couple more times. How is this possible? I must have been suffering from some kind of delirium because as I looked at the map I could see that all the station names had changed. I asked Brian, but he just stared, slack jawed and confused. I studied the names trying to make sense of them. They read "Blackboard gardens", "Market", "Rabbit Hole", "Abba". I had no idea what was going on and felt a sick nauseous feeling rise from my stomach to my mouth. Tears were stinging my eyes but as I looked around at the passengers they did not seem to notice.

"E-Excuse me" I said to a small middle aged woman. She turned and stared at me wide eyed with a look of fear which would have been more appropriate if I had just asked to buy her mother. "Excuse, uh, sorry to bother you" I stammered, the literal translation being "I don't trade in mothers, so please don't be afraid. But out of interest, how much would you sell her for anyway? No, I was just joking, please stop crying, it's ok. I'm sorry, uh, I'm an American!"

She brightened up a little and gave me a kindly smile, "Sure what is it?"

"Well, uh, I was wondering, uh, I mean, I lived here a couple of years ago and when I was here last the stations had completely different names, so, uh, I was wondering why that is?". The woman furrowed her brows and studied me for a while before saying "Well of course they've changed. I'm surprised you didn't know, it's been about 6 months. The new mayor, queer sort of fellow, decided it would be interesting to change the names of all the stations."

"But - but," I stammered, shocked yet mildly relieved that I hadn't imagined it, "That's completely absurd! I mean surely that would be completely confusing for the millions of tourists that visit this place?"

"Oh but they tell all the visitors before they get here. Didn't you get the notice on the plane?"

"No I did not!" Unless? I thought back. I remember being very drunk on the plane so perhaps the air stewards did give me something.

I reached into the pockets of my jacket which I had been wearing on the flight and took out a ruffled piece of paper. "Ah" I said as I read the notice which did in fact say "Notice to all visitors: The Mayor of London, queer sort of fellow, has decided it would be interesting to change the names of all the tube stations. To that end, please find enclosed a copy of the revised tube map." I thanked the woman with a spaced grin and she smiled widely at me. Then I winked at her which seemed to suggest that I actually would buy her mother if she offered her to me at a bargain discount due to the exchange rate of the pound against the dollar, which made the woman recoil a little and then she began to silently stare at another passenger. The other passengers who had been pretending not to listen looked after me as I got off at "Winehouse Way" with pure pity. I walked over to the tube map and luckily found that the format and colours of the tube lines remained the same and I could route my way to my destination; Fallen.

I floated onto the street, it was unchanged from my memories of it. Or maybe the place had changed however my memories had somehow changed in line with the physical. Perhaps I had grown with the place from across the pond. I tentatively walked up the street surveying the people around me walking past in technological bubbles. And then.

And then I saw this girl, bob hair cut bouncing along to her every step and I could feel every beat of my heart reverberate through my body. My darling, my blood. She looked completely out of place in her retro attire and deceptively nonchalant gaze, with an old woman's treasure of worries trying to hide behind her young eyes. She looks just like her mother I thought. She strolled on towards the traffic lights and automatically stopped at the red signal. She was now studying her MP3 player intently and changing from song to song to song. A symphony of beginnings. Still deep in thought as to what music would satisfy her heart at this very moment she walked past the cars without so much as glancing up and carried on walking down the street. Meanwhile, I followed her in the shadows. My heart was pulsating with excitement, "Just wait" I said to Brian, "Just wait until I speak to her, she won't believe it! She'll be angry, I'm sure, but eventually she'll be happy and the cosmos will fall into place. Just wait, I'll put everything right". And then.

Andrew and Ben of the Mayhem crew were turning the corner.

Their baggy jeans hanging low, their slow strides tinted with arrogance, they had the look of the fallen. Everything began to happen in slow motion, like when you are at the end of a quick sprint. You get to the finish line and at that moment the realisation hits. You realise then how far into the race you've run, how fast, with no opportunity to think it through or turn back. Andrew and Ben turned the corner and strode on.

I carried on following Val, working up the courage to tap her on the shoulder yet not knowing what I would say when she turned around. So maybe I need some help, ah yes, a prop, something to break the ice.

Val turned into the church and I followed. I hadn't been in a church in many years, the last time was probably before Val had been born. It wasn't deliberate, I had just got caught up in other things. I could see Val now, standing in front of that all famous figure, her head inclined slightly like a silhouette of Mother Mary. I walked softly around the right edge of the church and reached the front where I stood and stared at her, I saw a trickle of a tear rolling down her cheek. I continued to watch her, mesmerised, and reached into my pocket feeling around for my locket, a token of my love.

Andrew and Ben walked into the church and swaggered straight towards Val. I didn't even notice them at first and then when they were just behind Val I realised they were staring at her. A feeling of panic jolted into my chest. Val simply turned around slowly after casually wiping her eyes.

"So" her voice was soft but firm "I'm here as you asked and I've brought it"

Andrew's face turned into a sneer and Ben looked blankly ahead, almost robotic. "Do you fink dat's enough?" said Andrew, his shoulders spread out making him look bigger and more intimidating. "Dat's not how we work baby!" said Andrew, his sneer wider. "Yeah," chimed in Ben sucking his teeth and becoming more animated.

"A deal is a deal, now let him go ok!" Despite trying to control it, Val's voice was quavering giving her a slightly pleading quality "He didn't do anything to you, what the hell would he do, he's only three, so just end it here. I promise you I won't take it further. The money's here, look, count it if you want, just give me my brother back right now"

Brother? Where on earth did she get a brother from if her mother's dead and I certainly haven't got any kids? But I must confess those weren't the thoughts that were whizzing through my mind at that precise time.

"I've changed my mind" said Andrew, with a cruel smile of an all powerful ruler, "Come back tomorrow with double the money and you can have him back"

"I want to see him first, I want to make sure he's ok"

"He's fine" Andrew said laughing, "He's back at our flat playing playstation with my sister, so just chill the fuck out ok!"

"Tomorrow, at 3pm. And tell Ray he's a bastard"

Andrew smiled again, clearly enjoying Val's discomfort "Nah, he's my boy, I'll let you tell him, I don't get involved in lovers tiffs"

What was happening, I could not think. I had a gut wrenching urge to protect my Val, but Brian was telling me I should stay out of it as I would only make things worse. No, I would not interfere, I would simply stand here and watch. And yet, as I looked down at my feet my legs were carrying me forward. "Stop!" screamed Brian "What the hell are you doing? She's fine, she's handling it!" But my legs kept moving until I was within a metre of the shocked faces of Andrew, Ben and Val staring back at me. Val's expression was pure panic, as if I had returned to destroy everything. Andrew's face was contorted in anger and he began shouting about a set up and reaching around to the back of his jeans. The next thing I remember was the back of a gun smashing into my nose, and then darkness.

So, here I was, half dead in the church with my life flashing before my eyes, which was, let's face it, pretty convenient since you would never have known my story and the events leading up to my encounter with Val and her .... acquaintances. I felt my head which was throbbing in time with my heart, like a choir of bodily organs. I got to my knees and squinted at the cross before me and then slowly, and painfully, rested back on my legs and looked around the church, which was empty and ominously dark. I crawled towards the door and in the corner of my eye I could make out a shape on the floor by the pews on the other side of the church. My head was spinning but I got up and around me was darkness. I slowly walked down the pews, running my hand over the warm oak surface and steadying myself against its solid structure beneath the glare of his kind eyes. And there I saw her and stumbled towards her with my legs collapsing like matchsticks and the full weight of my body hit the hard stone floor.

Brian turned away, but I stared at her. There she was, strewn symmetrically across the ground like a snow angel, with specks of crimson on her beautiful face. A heart shaped wound on her chest, she almost looked graceful. She had a faint smile on her face and her eyes stared back at me, studying me intently from another world. An animalistic howl of anguish came from the back of my throat and tears were stinging my eyes. "Let's go" came Brian's quivering voice, "We can't stay here, the police will be on their way". So I reached my fingers to my lips and placed a kiss on Val's lips, and then unsteadily got to my feet and slowly walked out of the church with the sound of sirens in the background.

I knew that I was finished then. I walked into a pub and ordered a forgetting drink. I sipped the liquid fire and prayed for death, but it did not come, and would not come to absolve my sins. But what sins, I asked myself. Surely I had not sinned more than any other man. I had not cheated, I had not killed, I had lived a fairly ordinary yet selfish existence, but surely this was not bad enough to warrant purgatory. So what is my curse? I put my head into my hands and sighed deep and long for my dead child. But mainly I sighed for my lost self. I felt a sharp pain near my heart and clutched at my chest, and there I felt the locket in my breast pocket. My Soul! I took it out and examined the locket running my fingers over the surface. It looked as good as new. I opened the locket and saw the face I loved and also a ghostly face within staring back at me. I looked up at the barman with tears streaming down my cheeks and ordered another forgetting drink, trying to ignore the pity on his face. And then a jolt of lightning hit me and damn near sliced me in two for I realised that I was back in a reincarnated version of the pub I had worked at those many years ago. The very place I had met Mandy, the very place which had vaporised into a million atoms and began the story of our love. Love. I had now found my sin, I found that I had come full circle and found the answer to the puzzle of my lost self; I bring sorrow to those that love me. Such has come to pass and such will come to be.

The Archivist

He drifted down the corridor, impervious to the clients and lawyers marching in the other direction. He looked at the wallpaper peeling from the walls and felt grateful to the dreadful portraits which were preserving at least some of the walls' dignity.

He floated down the stairs. The lamps were dim and an unnerving gloominess engulfed him as he reached the basement door. But now was not the time to be afraid for he needed that deed and he reached out for the rusty door handle.

Suddenly the basement door swung open of its own accord. He peered into the darkness and with trepidation took his first steps into the black void. It had obviously been expecting him. He instinctively reached for light and with luck found a dusty electric lantern by his feet. A surge of ecstasy seemed to run through his now cold blood as he realised that the lantern worked and he could see down the stairs. A cold concrete basement stared up at him. His heavy bones creaked down the worn stairs and as he reached the bottom of the staircase an array of large filing cabinets towered over him. The suffocating musty smell of paper was almost too much to bear so he loosened his tie, unbuttoned his shirt collar and took in deep panic breaths as if breathing under water.

And so he slowly walked towards the far end of the basement gripped by an irrational fear that each step could be his last. He arrived at his destination; a lone cabinet beside the far wall, and as he stopped he could feel the cabinets behind him move together to block his entrance and stare ominously into his back.

His hands trembling with fear, he opened the cabinet and was astounded by what he saw; a human heart, bathed in an intense white glow which seemingly lit the entire basement with enough light to illuminate the world seven times over. What was even stranger, he realised with a stab, was that the heart was beating, it was alive!

"Why?" he cried. Behind him the cabinets shuddered only to stop when he swung around with unexpected bravery.

He turned back to face the pulsating redness, smug in its now effervescent glow.

"I don't understand?" He could not hide the desperation in his voice.

Without warning the cabinet doors behind him began to violently open and shut. The combination of the deafening noise and penetrating light had now driven him to nausea and, tear stricken, he reached into the cabinet and grabbed the throbbing heart in his hand, staring at it with his deep wide eyes. The cabinets stopped and watched him in anticipation.

"And so it has come to this!", and without another word he closed his eyes, put the heart into his mouth and bit down. The heart's throbbing began to seep into his body until he was shaking, but still his resolve was strong and he patiently chewed the life out of the heart until all that was left was a metallic taste in his tired mouth.

Slowly he opened his eyes and looked around the basement which had hitherto been a haunting dark place yet now seemed the very epitome of mundane. His pulse was racing and his feet seemed to have left the ground.

After the many years of solitary confinement in this bleak servitude, a smile faintly broke onto his face for the first time and as he sat down on the cold concrete floor a warm sensation engulfed him. He wiped the blood away and started to laugh.

The Hundredth Soul

It was a Sunday just like any other and Leroy Stockwell was sitting in his kitchen listening to his radio whilst reading the morning paper. A perfectly normal day, a perfectly normal life. Predictable worries filled his head; what colour to paint his garage, whether pro-active margarine actually made any difference to his cholesterol, you know, the normal sort of thing. Suddenly Leroy had a vision of the recurring nightmare that had plagued him. He could see himself running down a corridor, his feet pounding on the cold concrete floor, his heart in his throat, "Get out" something was screaming at him. The corridor was pale white with dim lamps on the wall. He saw the outline of a grand ornate door shimmering somewhere between his dream and waking. Leroy ran and ran through the corridor until he abruptly snapped out of his reverie and was back in his kitchen.

Leroy chomped down on his toast thoughtfully and ran his fingers across the corner of his newspaper until the corner gently willed to his direction and curled over. "Surges of electric energy confuses livestock" read the headline. Leroy blinked a couple of times to let the day in and a consortium of bizarre headlines, marmalade and the promise of the new day marched into his tired eyes, giving him a gentle push into wakefulness. Leroy heard a rustling and looked up, starting a little as he saw his cousin standing before him.

They stared at each other across the breakfast table. Leroy's cousin, Daniel, had an odd contrasting face consisting of a mischievous smirk yet deep meaningful eyes. "Uh hi" Leroy finally said as Daniel sat himself down at the kitchen table and began buttering some toast. "How are you?" asked Daniel as he carefully spread the margarine with deft flicks of his hand. That was typical of Daniel, thought Leroy, he was always straight. Straight to the point with everything with no room for unnecessary words or detours. "Oh, I'm ok thanks" came Leroy's bland response. But he wasn't ok. He was lying through his marmalade stained teeth to the most honest person he had ever known. His job was a joke. Not so much a joke as a parody of someone else's life. It was as if his entire existence was the product of some in-joke of which he was not aware. He worked, well actually he surfed the internet all day whilst consuming vast quantities of coffee, at a large specialist fraud practice.

He was one of the junior accountants there to count other people's money and marvel at how creative they had been in selling pyramid schemes to people who were far too intelligent to fall for them. Most of all, he marvelled at how he could get through the entire day without punching the moron at the desk next to him. When he got home he would invariably sit in his flat, alone with the TV, pondering which exotic location he would move to when he had saved enough money. But "I'm ok thanks" seemed to be the standard response. Daniel stared deep into Leroy making him shift uncomfortably in his chair, he wasn't buying it. "I want to take you somewhere" said Daniel, his pure eyes now alive with some magical energy, and Leroy could not refuse.

Leroy and Daniel were standing in an empty tube carriage holding onto the poles and swinging slightly to the rhythm of the train. Leroy casually looked up at the tube map, studying the stations that they were passing, when suddenly he felt a deep surge of panic in his throat. Leroy realised that they had passed Chancery Lane station, where he worked, and the train was now moving forward with an almost egotistical speed, somehow accelerated on by the fuel of Leroy's ascending panic. "Shit!" exclaimed Leroy, "I'm going to be late". Daniel, who was looking dreamily at the posters, shook his head and calmly replied "No we won't".

"Of course we, I mean *I* will, I've just missed my station!", a moment of realisation set in, "Wait, where exactly are we going?", Leroy could hear the slightly hysterical note to his voice.

"To the end of the line" said Daniel as he strolled to the last seat of the carriage and sat down. Leroy walked over and sat next to him, immediately regretting not leaving a couple of seats space between them, and each stared ahead at the other's reflection until Leroy looked away first, embarrassed.

Daniel was freakishly tall and lean, with an athletic quality about him like a basketball player. Which, incidentally, he was. He played professional basketball, if such a thing exists in Britain, and when he wasn't playing ball he would read his books or creepily appear in his cousin's flat and adultnap him from work. Well actually that only happened just this once. Leroy was impressed at the stretch of Daniel's legs and the general imposing quality of his presence. Leroy had played basketball with him a couple of times, when he dared, and was always intimidated as soon as Daniel strolled onto the court. Leroy compared his own scrawny body in the dim light of the train until the next stop propelled him from his self examination. Daniel gave a slight shake of his head to say "not there yet" and closed his eyes.

A few stations later the train held at the platform for longer than usual and Leroy suddenly had a sickening feeling he could not explain. He looked ahead, his eyes transfixed at the seats before him, and he heard a slight squeak on the arm rest on the seat in front. Then he saw the seat groove slightly as if someone had just sat down. Leroy continued to stare straight ahead and felt shivers like a thousand hungry spiders running up and down his body.

Daniel awoke with a start from his slumber and saw the terrified expression on Leroy's face. Leroy then saw that Daniel was now staring at the same seat; eyes wide and alert as if ready to strike. Leroy looked ahead and noticed that he could not see his own reflection in the window only a human shaped silhouette, but could clearly make out Daniel's face to his left, eyes burning like fire. Suddenly the next station arrived and as the doors opened the groove in the seat disappeared and Daniel's eyes followed the seemingly invisible being out until the doors had closed. Leroy let out a loud abrupt laugh at how ridiculous they were both being, however, as he met Daniel's cold hard expression Leroy's levity dissipated and he decided that if he was an invisible being who randomly sat on trains he would also have left the carriage immediately. Leroy also decided that he would not watch any more horror movies late on work nights because his lines between reality and illusion were evidently now blurring beyond all hope of rescue.

They reached Epping station in silence, with Leroy now feeling much like the invisible man. Leroy stared at the throngs of people outside the ticket booth on their way to work. As he should be. "Shit!" Leroy had another minor panic attack when he thought about how much trouble he would be in and decided to call in sick for work. They walked for a while down the lacklustre streets and Leroy studied Daniel as he strolled on almost in a trance.

Leroy dialled the number, "Uh hello?" no that doesn't sound sick enough, "Uuuhh *cough* hello?", needs more practice thought Leroy, when suddenly he heard a voice on the other end of the phone. "Oh uh hi Martin, how are you?" Why am I asking him how he is, Leroy despaired, *I'm* supposed to be calling in sick! Martin was Leroy's immediate manager and whilst Leroy got on with him he had a rather cold telephone manner which resulted in Leroy always asking if he was alright. "Leroy, I take it you're not coming in?" came Martin's unfeeling telephone response, "uh- no I'm sick" Leroy replied, feeling like a child. "Hope to see you tomorrow" said Leroy and hung up the phone, immediately feeling alone and scared. Leroy could see that Daniel was smirking a little and found this dry telephone exchange rather humourous.

Leroy began to feel a dull ache in his head in the space between his eyes, which was evolving into a persistent throbbing. He squinted at the passing cars and people as he slowly walked on. The aching was getting worse as he walked, as if his body was warning him to turn back. "Daniel", Leroy could barely talk as his voice came out in a desperate whisper, "Where are we going?". Daniel carried on striding forward and impassively replied "To the end of the street". "Of course we are" muttered Leroy under his breath, suddenly realising that despite his throbbing head, conflicting emotions and sore body, his overwhelming feeling was still curiosity.

Eventually they reached a building, and now the pain inside Leroy's head was screaming at him to turn back and run for his life. He looked up at the grand architecture of an old converted church which stood proudly before him. Daniel stepped up to the large oak door, gingerly grabbed the old fashioned door knock and knocked three times. And three times the knocks resonated through the building, as if waking it from its slumber. Now the building stood over them, majestic and imposing and a chill shot down Leroy's spine. Suddenly the door opened and a kindly woman looked out at them with overly happy squinting eyes and a wide grin. "Ah Daniel", she kissed him on both cheeks and looked over at Leroy, "This must be Leroy", Daniel nodded and walked in with Leroy following, unsure of himself in the squinty woman's overt joy at the world. And yet, as she looked into his eyes and Leroy walked into the darkness of the building, the pain disappeared.

Leroy looked around and saw a hub of around 200 people standing in the middle of the large hall. They were drinking wine and talking whilst gesticulating animatedly to each other. The hall had retained its old fashioned design and Leroy peered up at the stained glass windows and the bright benevolent eyes of the saints smiled back at him. On either side of the hall were empty stalls. A few of the people stopped talking when Leroy and Daniel entered. "What are they doing here?", a loud voice boomed from somewhere at the back and suddenly the room went quiet and the people turned to watch the newcomers like some eerie school assembly. Leroy faced the crowd which parted and walking towards them was a man with the look of a sage but, as it seemed to Leroy, the manner of a city trader. "I came to see his Holiness Ninety Nine" replied the unfazed Daniel. The sagacious looking man had long wild white hair with big bushy eyebrows and a shaggy beard. Although his face had a naturally kind look, his mouth was curled into a sneer and his eyes were sharp, "I thought you refused to be part of this". "Oh leave them be, anyone is welcome in the market, you know that George" said the kind squinty eyed lady and Leroy shot her a warm smile, grateful for some support in the midst of the collectively suspicious stare of a few hundred pairs of eyes. Daniel and George stood before each other in a hostile staring match and Leroy shuffled nervously wanting the ground to swallow him up.

Suddenly an exquisitely beautiful woman with a huge mane of red hair walked briskly past them through the gathering and rang an old fashioned bell at the far end of the hall. "And let the trading begin" she cried and at once the crowd dispersed into sections and gathered around the stalls as if they were at a school fete. However, upon closer inspection Leroy realised that nothing was physically being sold at some of the stalls and people were simply gathered around them. Daniel and Leroy casually strolled past the stalls observing the musical bartering around them. "I need three quarters of invisibility", said one slightly hysterical woman, a muffled response, "Never mind why! Are you going to sell it to me or not?", another muffled response, "No, I'm not going to commit any crime, I just *need* it". A long pause came. "I…" the woman's voice now quiet, "I don't want my husband to see where I'm going", and at that she shook hands with the air and Leroy rather suspected that she was insane and quickly moved to another stall.

As he walked he noticed a grandly ornate spiral staircase. At the bottom of the staircase was a secretary seated in front of a low office desk upon which was a rather large black box. Her small oval glasses perched on her nose and her forehead was furrowed in concentration as she read through the sodden pages spread out before her on the desk. The secretary began typing words into the large black box and as she tapped water splashed out from the box all over her and the desk. Leroy walked closer and saw that the black box was filled with water and as he peered over he saw that inside the water there sat a keyboard. The secretary paid no mind to Leroy and typed and splashed away with such normality that after a little while Leroy couldn't imagine that typing sounded like anything other than splashing water.

"How can that possibly be a fair price?" shouted one ruffled man at George as he pushed his way out of the crowd surrounding George's stall. Leroy saw the man walking away defiantly at first and then slowly he transformed giving in to his weakness, his principles wilting until finally he slowly sunk into himself and then, half the man that he was to start with, he heavily made his way back through the crowd to George's stall. Leroy followed and pushed his way through the crowd until before him he saw the man standing in front of George, their eyes locked as if they were about to draw guns at dawn. George's face was full of contempt and arrogance, "OK" said the man slowly, "I will buy a quarter". "Somehow Matthew, I thought you might" George smiled and handed over a small glass bottle filled with a thick black liquid, which looked like blackstrap molasses, and Matthew drank it down greedily. George handed over a small piece of paper, "I do wish you would at least glance at the prescription before consuming it whole". Matthew was unsteady on his feet but his face was a picture of pure blank ecstasy. Matthew sank to the ground and began to giggle, much to the amusement of the crowd. Meanwhile, George completed the transaction on some old fashioned parchment after which he tore the bottom half of it and handed it to Matthew. "As we agreed, payment will be in five instalments, one a week, which will be taken with the other payments owed by you." "Yes, yes" came Matthew's feeble voice as he curled up into the foetal position, tears rolling down his eyes, "I just want the pain to go away".

Leroy kept looking at Matthew, every ounce of his being was telling him to stop staring to give Matthew some of his dignity back, but something deep inside Leroy, and indeed inside the gathered crowd, took pleasure in this humiliation. And then a few more in the crowd took their bottles from George, and scrunched the prescriptions in their hands as they consumed the black liquid. Leroy decided to walk around and inspect the other stalls which seemed to consist of various people talking to each other. Upon closer inspection he saw that each stall had a name, one was called Wisdom, another called Debate, another called Entertainment, yet George's stall, Medicine, was by far the busiest.

Suddenly the stunning red haired woman rang her bell and the group immediately stopped talking and turned to face the spiral staircase at the front of the building. Daniel looked noticeably on edge which in turn made Leroy very uneasy. Faint footsteps began to echo through the silence and Leroy saw a pair of glossy black shoes, the trouser end of a pin stripe suit and a rather fetching silk cloak make their way down the steps. The traditionally stylish attire then slowly transformed into an elegant man with pitch black hair, a long nose, manic eyes and a slightly crooked smile. On his chest hung a rather ostentatious medallion in the shape of '99', which Leroy figured must have made him his Holiness Ninety Nine. Leroy felt rather smug at having figured that out and looked over at Daniel, however Daniel had left his side and was now skulking in the corner of the room looking glum and staring intensely at Ninety Nine. "Greetings", his voice was deep and authoritative, "it is now time for the transmission" and at that the crowd instinctively walked towards the centre of the room and gathered in a perfectly formed circle, as if in some kind of trance, and stared up at some fixed point at the centre of the ceiling. Leroy could see now that they were staring at an inverted pyramid pointing down towards them. He noticed the black pyramid was covered in gold lettering with what looked like ancient scriptures. He then looked down and saw Ninety Nine staring at him with those unnerving dark manic eyes which made Leroy instantly uncomfortable. Ninety Nine smiled his crooked smile at Leroy and then proceeded to address the crowd, "Now would the congregation raise their right hands and be ready to transmit and feed" and at that the crowd pointed their hands up towards the pyramid and, following a countdown from the red haired lady, a myriad of dazzling beams of white light made their way from the pointed fingers of the gathering towards the pyramid's point. Across the top of the beams Leroy saw small red lightning strikes creeping along the white beams of light until they climbed onto the congregation's fingers and then ran up and down their bodies.

With an almighty bang the light disappeared and the members of the gathering collapsed onto the floor, exhausted. Leroy walked over to Daniel who was sat on the floor with his back rested against the far wall, a look of pity in his eyes as he studied the members of the crowd trying to regain their strength. Leroy could see from the corner of his eye that the manic eyes were still on him. "That is singularly the weirdest thing I have ever seen", he announced. "I don't know, the squirrel artist is rather strange" said a voice behind him, Leroy jumped and saw nothing there, "What the!"

"Oh, sorry, how rude", a woman appeared before him. She had absurd quaffed blonde hair, which only people with powers of invisibility must be able to get away with, Leroy thought, and punk clothes complete with braces hanging against her bondage pants. "Hi" she smiled widely at him and outstretched her hand to shake his, "My name is Veronica". Leroy looked uneasily at her hand and Veronica giggled with childish glee, "It's alright, you won't get electrocuted, it just lasts a couple of seconds after the transmission" and Leroy took her hand into his and gently shook it feeling instantly at ease in her company. "So, what's this squirrel artist?" asked Leroy, Veronica smiled again, "Oh it's a squirrel in Hyde Park who draws pictures of passers by, he's very good". Leroy smiled at her, "Well, you'll have to show me one day", and Veronica nodded and then looked at the floor nervously, "Oh my God!" thought Leroy, mortified, "Why am I flirting with her?". He looked over at Daniel who could not hide the amusement in his eyes and then, with horror, realised that he was still holding onto Veronica's hand. "Oh sorry" Leroy withdrew his hand and, feeling his cheeks flushing red, he started to back away from her.

Leroy suddenly felt a prickle on the hairs on his neck and turning swiftly around he saw the grand presence of his Holiness Ninety Nine standing before him. "Well hello," he leered, "I see we have a new presence at our gathering, as well as some old and unexpected attendance" he shot Daniel a condescending look, "And what do we owe the honour of your presence here today Daniel?". Daniel slowly looked up, "The honour belongs to my cousin, Leroy", a triumphant smile spread across Daniel's face, "He is the Hundredth Soul".

Ninety nine's face clouded and his eyes filled with oozing blackness "The what?". Daniel smiled, "As you know it was prophesised that the

Hundredth Soul would be revealed this month, and I have located him". "*He* is the Hundredth Soul?" sneered Ninety Nine, "This gag reel of a human being, this meandering puddle along the road to the benefits office? Prove it!". Daniel calmly walked over to the mystified Leroy, reached for his right hand and rolled his sleeve up, and there was his arm like any other arm save for a few scratches from his mother's new emotionally disturbed cat. He lifted Leroy's hand up vertically and there appeared on his wrist a small black symbol. When he was younger Leroy had often pretended that his small pyramid shaped birthmark was of great significance in his own private adventure movie but as he got older it only ever became a conversation point with strangers and was generally slightly creepy to girlfriends. Eyes wide with horror, Ninety Nine grabbed Leroy's wrist and inspected the mark trying to rub it out with his cloak. Upon realising that the mark was real Ninety Nine stormed off and disappeared into a room at the north end of the hall, much to Daniel's amusement.

"What was that about? And what the hell is a hundredth soul?", Leroy looked from Daniel to Veronica now feeling like more of an outcast. Veronica was staring open mouthed at Leroy, "Wait a second, *you're* the Hundredth Soul, on my god, I can't believe it!" she turned to Daniel "is he really? Is he going to change the course of our society, of the Gifted?" Daniel nodded sagely and then reached out and grabbed Leroy's arm "I think we need to have a little chat".

Out in the open air Leroy could feel chills of the unwelcoming wind running through his bones, he walked quickly on, away from Daniel, hoping that some space from Daniel's world would help to make some sense of these unusual events. Daniel ran up and placed his arm around Leroy's back just as he had done when they were boys. Leroy recalled this gesture from Daniel whenever Leroy had been teased by his classmates and Daniel would invariably make things worse by sticking up for him. Daniel leaned in to whisper into Leroy's ear "He's going to kill you". Leroy stopped dead as if he had been hit by a bolt of lightening "What?", his voice was faint. "I said", Daniel's expression was completely factual, devoid of emotion as if he was telling Leroy he had run out of milk, "I said, he's going to kill you". "Oh, well, that's ok, for a second there it sounded like something terrible!", Leroy's heart was pounding and beads of sweat were accumulating around his upper lip for he knew exactly who Daniel was referring to, "I don't want to inconvenience you or anything Dan but would you mind telling me exactly why he's going to kill me". Daniel positioned himself directly in front of Leroy and put one hand on each of his shoulders "Yes certainly, but first we have to get out of here quickly, so you need to teleport us somewhere now". Despite the imminence of his death Leroy began to giggle wildly and felt jolts of nervous joy dancing with the tremors of fear throughout his body, resulting in highly a pleasant sensation. Daniel gently shook Leroy by his shoulders, "Look, I know it must all seem odd to you because you've forgotten everything but I know you have it as your gift". Daniel's panicked eyes began searching around trying to find some way to convince Leroy, "I remember you did it once when we were eight and we landed in that field and had to walk home for 5 miles, do you remember that?". Seeing Daniel's pleading eyes before him Leroy stopped laughing and tried to piece together the confusion in his mind. He remembered getting lost with his cousin and ending up in a field when they were around eight, and remembered the blisters in his feet from the long walk home. He felt the surge of the familiar feeling of somehow 'landing' in a field but his sepia toned childhood memories usually contained a preponderance of feelings as opposed to actual events. He closed his eyes to get away from the panic at what Daniel was telling him and away from insane things which had happened that day and tried to imagine he was in the field which they had got lost in all those years ago. He visualised the farm bathed in sunlight; the endless greens, browns and yellows, the shy cows, the elegant horses, the towering trees and the nearby stream from where they had drank on their long walk back home. Leroy now felt entirely peaceful as the cool breeze ran through his hair and then a flash. Before he opened his eyes he knew exactly where he had taken Daniel.

"Thanks" Daniel walked over to the stream and Leroy silently collapsed onto the moist grass taking in his surroundings. Daniel cupped some water in his hands and splashed it over his face, "I know this must all seem like a shock to you after the insect circus but your gift is innate and not something you can forget completely." "I'm sorry, what? The insect circus?", Daniel looked over at Leroy who was now lying flat on the grass staring up at the grey clouds, "Well, it doesn't matter now, all I'm saying is that you never forget. Listen Leroy, it's getting cold now mate so let's start walking towards that farmhouse" Leroy was in a daze staring up at the sky and Daniel was fading away from his peripheral vision. Then suddenly Leroy was somehow face down lying on a cloud peeping through the white cotton at the world beneath. He saw Daniel walking slowly towards the farmhouse and his own lowly figure getting up from the grass and following behind.

Leroy's legs were heavy as he followed Daniel towards the farmhouse in the distance. A thousand confused thoughts were frantically running through his mind, shouting down his certain thoughts, as if in some chaotic parliamentary debate, until all his confused and certain thoughts were muddled into certain confusion. "My name is Leroy", he whispered to himself, "My name is Leroy". Suddenly a butterfly flew straight into Leroy's face and fluttered there before him in slow motion as Leroy's subconscious was invoked with every flap of the butterfly's wings, one flap, two, three.

Leroy is ten years old staring at a butterfly in the magnified glass box. It is pink with black stripes and it's antenna are moving around frantically as it perches on a metal hoop over a miniature trampoline. The insect circus. Leroy remembers his parents had taken him and Daniel there as a special treat for doing well at school. They had walked up to the old fashioned red and black wagon covered in garish gold paintings of ladybugs and horseflies and as they walked to the entrance an old man with a bandana and toothy grin welcomed them into the wagon. Leroy's parents paid the old man and ushered for Leroy and Daniel to step in saying they would wait outside. Going up the stairs Leroy looked back and saw his mother whisper something to the old man who nodded and said "I give you my word, and as you know my word is my bond".

It is now dark in the wagon and the only lights are the ones below the glass boxes, which Daniel and Leroy are peering into, showing the insects in various circus acts. Across the room they notice a partition protected by a heavy old red curtain peppered with stains. The old man enters and smiles his toothy smile at Daniel and Leroy saying that behind the curtain is the main attraction, something they could never imagine in their wildest dreams. He says that he can only allow one at a time and Daniel and Leroy fight over who will go first. Leroy has won their diplomatic game of rock, paper, scissors and Daniel sulkily stands with the insects pretending he is not the slightest bit interested in what is behind the curtain. As he steps through Leroy sees a kindly old woman seated behind a table upon which stands a large crystal shard. She smiles at him and takes him by the hand "Don't worry son, your gift cannot be extinguished and your parents are fools for thinking it can be" she grins at Leroy's confused expression "but I can make you forget it for a little while", and with that she clicks her fingers and everything has gone blank. The next thing Leroy remembers is being led out of the wagon and his mother giving him a big hug "Did you enjoy the insect circus darling?" and Leroy doesn't have the foggiest idea. He looks around for Daniel "Oh, he ran home saying he didn't want to see the insects" his mother smiled. Leroy giggles to himself since he had never expected Daniel to be a coward and for the rest of the day he walks tall and proud, as the insect circus master.

The butterfly's wings brought him back and Leroy was now walking rhythmically behind Daniel who, with long confident strides, was now nearing the farmhouse. Leroy felt a strange urge to be near his cousin so he bounded towards him until they were walking side by side with Daniel slowing down his pace so that Leroy could keep up. "Listen, I have so many things to tell you, but I'm hungry and tired and I think we need to rest a little while", Leroy nodded and they walked silently on.

Daniel knocked urgently on the farmhouse's door, however there was no answer. The farmhouse was protected by a frame of large overgrown bushes and broken wooden gate. Leroy surveyed the messy exterior and peered through the grimy window, Daniel knocked again and again but there was no hint of anyone inside the house. "Hello?", the house was silent. Leroy observed some buckets and mops strewn untidily across the front yard and no animals around, which was highly unusual for a farmhouse. Daniel reached down and pried loose one of the bricks making up the front doorstep. Before Leroy could stop him Daniel had smashed the brick through the window and Leroy ran into the bushes, the imaginary screech of police sirens playing in his head. Daniel looked over at Leroy's cowering stance and smirked as he calmly reached his arm through the broken window to unlock the latch and carefully pulled the window up making sure he did not cut himself on the broken glass. Leroy walked slowly towards Daniel whilst looking around for Farmer Gray and his two hounds from hell to jump out of the bushes and apprehend them. "What the *hell* are you doing?" Leroy's voice was high pitched and ridiculous again. "Seriously Dan, this is someone's house. I mean, you can't just break their window and climb in, I could have just teleported us somewhere else or something, I mean does the phrase 'breaking and entering' mean anything to you?" Daniel's torso was now inside the farmhouse and his legs were sticking straight out, as if the house was swallowing him, then his feet slowly disappeared into the window. Leroy felt quite empty all of a sudden as he stood there stupefied on the front yard. Daniel's head poked out of the window "Are you coming or what?", Leroy stood firmly with his arms folded staring at Daniel sulkily. "There's food here", Leroy's sulking gave way to the painful hunger in his stomach and he finally made his way into the farmhouse via the broken window.

Leroy was seated at the dinner table in a musty living room having just finished a hearty meal of cold tinned food stew and some sweet wine, which Daniel had found on his expedition to the back rooms and cellar. His eyes were fixed on Daniel who was seated in the chair in front, his body with perfect posture, his hands clasped together in front of him and his face the very definition of tranquil. "So" Daniel began, "I will now explain it all. His Holiness Ninety Nine wants to kill you because I told him that you are the Hundredth Soul". Leroy nodded, "I got that part", Daniel continued "And the reason he wants to kill you is because the Hundredth Soul will succeed him to the throne as the ruler of all of us," Leroy's head was hurting again, "the Gifted. There are thousands of us all over the world and we connect with each other through the internet and at various local group meetings such as the one we just went to at the headquarters in London. His Holiness Ninety Nine is the ninety ninth soul who is capable of leading the Gifted in return for us paying a tax on our gifts. The Great Souls such as Ninety Nine are immortal, with one exception, in that they can only be killed by another Great Soul. So, to protect his position as the Leader, Ninety Nine will kill you. What's so funny about that?" Leroy did not know why but he was smiling. On his face was a big stupid smile at the sheer ridiculousness of what he was being told. "Oh nothing, this all just seems perfectly normal, why wouldn't it? Do continue". Daniel blinked and stared unresponsively at Leroy's lame sarcasm, "You need to remember to teleport. It's important that you practice and practice until it becomes second nature to you. He will attempt to find you wherever in the world you are. His ministers have a range of gifts that he will use to locate you; invisibility, flight, and teleporting". Leroy nodded, still smiling like an idiot "Right, so basically, I'm fucked". Daniel suppressed a smile, "Not exactly. It's just that if you ever come face to face with Ninety Nine, get yourself out of there immediately, no matter what's going on."

Suddenly they heard a soft creak on the floorboards and Daniel swung around towards the corridor ready to fight the intruder. There was nobody there, no sound, just the beat of Leroy's heart. Daniel was on edge, like a big cat ready to pounce. They sat there, still as palm trees in the desert, eyes surveying the room and corridor outside. "Vermeer" shouted Daniel into the air "I know it's you, show yourself you coward!". Silence continued to fill the room "Show yourself", and at that a rather expensive looking vase by the fireplace at the end of the room began to topple over. Without a moment's hesitation Daniel swung around on his heels and an arrow of fire shot out from his hand sending pieces of ceramic vase flying through the room. Leroy was cowering on the floor with his hands on his face. He could feel wood and glass shattering into a hundred pieces and showering him as Daniel continued to fire into the void. Leroy heard a fragile cry ringing through the broken furniture "Wait!", Daniel stopped firing when he saw Leroy's expression and listened into the spaces, "Wait", it was a female voice, "It's me". Leroy surveyed the empty room, "Veronica?". A faint outline of a human appeared beside the dinner table and there crouched was Veronica, eyes wide with fear, picking out pieces of the vase from her hair. Daniel let out a groan then stomped over to the armchair by the fireplace and, sweeping away the rubble with hands, he sat down and stared daggers into Veronica. "What the hell are you doing here?" Veronica looked away back to Leroy and bent her head down in embarrassment, "I followed you, but I didn't mean to".

"What?", Leroy realised his high pitched girl's voice was about to encore, "how could you have followed us from the gathering? And what do you mean you *didn't mean to*? How can you accidentally follow someone from Epping to a farm in, in God knows where, without meaning to?" Veronica looked from Leroy to Daniel, who was now seated at the armchair eying Veronica with undisguised contempt. "Ok,

I can explain. I *did* mean to follow you when you left the gathering, I was just so amazed that you are the Hundredth Soul that I followed, unthinking" she looked deep into Leroy's eyes and continued "I saw you both walking down the street and then you stopped for no apparent reason and Daniel put his hands on your shoulders, so I walked up until I was right behind Daniel. But then you closed your eyes and began to meditate or something, so I thought I'd slip my business card into Daniel's pocket so that if you wanted to contact me you could". She suddenly looked sheepish realising what she had just said, "Anyway, so, suddenly I found myself with both of you in the field. I didn't want to reveal myself to you because I thought you'd be angry and, well, you know, I was obviously right". She stopped waiting for some reassurance from Leroy but none came and Daniel continued to eye her suspiciously.

Leroy sank into a rather uncomfortable chair and immediately felt a heavy weight on his eyelids forcing him to sink into darkness. He could still make out the guilty expression on Veronica's face and could see the outline of Daniel reclining on the armchair in front of him, but the shapes were melting into each other and soon Leroy was asleep.

There was a flurry of activity behind Leroy's eyelids, chairs moving, a gentle murmuring of voices, banging pots and pans, scraping plates. Leroy was in the garden of his childhood, riding around on his beloved, if lethally dangerous, 'Chopper' bike. Pure freedom, pure everything, it was his own personal heaven. "Lee, honey come in, tea" he heard his mother's voice sweeping through the cool breeze tickling his ears. He parked his bike next to the wall and stepped into the kitchen where his mother was busy stirring some delicious stew in their big pot. Leroy smiled contently as he let the rich aroma fill his lungs and casually strolled into the living room where his father was watching Countdown on the television. Suddenly young Leroy could see his adult self in the television running down a dark corridor and soon his nightmare had superimposed itself onto his idyllic vision of utopia and the familiar panic surged into him like an electric shock making his body freeze into submission. Leroy felt his tired legs running down a claustrophobic dimly lit corridor. The panic was consuming him and a tumult of voices were ringing in his ears telling him to get out of there. At length he reached a slightly open grand oak door. From the crack in the door he saw an elegant ceremonial candle peeking through. The candle began to force its way through forming six gangly leg shapes and one terrifying fang shape which then spilt up into thousands of miniature versions of the absurd spidery wax creature and crawled speedily towards him. Before he had time to turn and run two spiders had crawled up his legs and onto his shoulders. Leroy had one spider on each shoulder and suddenly, rather inexplicably, they fastened their legs tight and began jerking his shoulders back and forth with all the strength of a human being.

Leroy awoke to see Daniel in front of him, his powerful hands withdrawing from his shoulders, his face a picture of calm in the dim room. Leroy was hungry and the three of them sat down at the table and ate breakfast like some twisted family. It was still dark outside which made Leroy feel a little uneasy. Daniel and Veronica looked at Leroy expectantly and Leroy felt a sudden surge of incompetence "I think we should take the train back, it's … it's not what they would expect". Daniel looked at Leroy the way a parent would regard a failing child, "Ok, but in that case we won't go back, we'll go somewhere else".

The three of them took their own four seat section in the empty chugging train. Leroy gazed out of the window at the expanse of countryside in the frame of daybreak. He stared, mesmerised, at the green fields and small blue lagoons. A mystical fog settled on the ground and water and Leroy felt he was in a dream. The deep orange glow of the sun beamed across the mist and stayed there above the treetops, reflected in the supernatural blue. Leroy could see the mist slowly melting into skies so that he could not tell where the mist stopped and clouds began. An image of oblivion before him.

And then Leroy awoke from a chugging train induced sleep. Or had been awake in some trance like state and had somehow managed to navigate onto the tube with Daniel and Veronica before him, staring at him with curious concern. Leroy's ears and sinuses were blocked and all he could hear was a quiet ringing in his ears. He viewed the tube map, "We're heading towards Kentish town", said Daniel, but Leroy's ears were blocked and Daniel's voice was quiet and muffled.

They finally reached a quaint antique bookshop and Leroy stared up with admiration at the cornucopia of the leather bound jewels which adorned the dusty window. The front door had a 'closed' sign so Daniel rang the front door bell and the three of them shuffled around for a while as nobody answered the door. Leroy observed a spider nonchalantly crawling towards some unfortunate fly which had managed to tangle itself up in its web, Veronica studied the cracks in the floor and Daniel incessantly rang the bell like an obstinate child, growing more impatient by the minute. "Well hello there!" came a voice behind them and the three swung around in surprise. "Bloody hell Herm!" cried out Daniel, ashamed at having been caught off guard, "We've been waiting here for ages, I thought it was supposed to start at three?".

'Herm' was a tall handsome young man with exquisite golden brown skin and a cheeky wide smile. He wore ripped jeans and a baseball cap which covered wisps of wavy dark hair. He deftly began to unlock the numerous locks and made way for the three of them to enter, shifting piles of books and trying to make the corridor into the bookshop seem less of an assault course, "This way, my friends, this way! Yes you are indeed right, Danny my boy, it is supposed to start at three. And right now it's a quarter to, so we have 15 whole minutes, an eternity!" Herm led them to a flight of stairs which led down to the basement as a puzzled Daniel listened to his watch and flicked his wrist a couple of times in the air in the vain hope that this action would fix it. Leroy and Veronica exchanged quizzical looks as Herm bounded down the stairs offering a cup of tea into space. They looked back at Daniel who was still frowning at his watch, and then decided to take their first courageous steps into the dimly lit basement. As they reached the bottom Leroy became aware that they were actually in a fairly large hall in the guise of a basement. The hall was all white and illuminated by large outdoor lamps. Each of its four walls contained a long bookshelf filled with rows and rows of old books, and the aroma of leather, antique dust and incense drifted around them. Towards the middle centre of the hall to the front of the stairs was a gathering of people, a motley crew of young and old alike, sitting cross legged on the floor in large circles. At the far end of the hall was a young woman seated in front of a large organ, hands poised in anticipation.

Suddenly Leroy sensed the patter of footsteps down the basement stairs and a tall female figure in a flowing white robe-like dress brushed past them and walked towards the circles where she found a spot on the edge and sat crossed legged on the floor. She had long shiny hair, wide eyes, and a serenely beautiful face at which Leroy couldn't help but stare. Herm casually strolled towards them from a trolley at the far end of the hall carrying a tray with three cups of steaming tea. He smiled at them as he handed the cups out and took off his baseball cap revealing a crown of silky hair. "We're all ready to start, your Excellency", called out one of the attendees, "I'll be right there" replied Herm as he handed out the tea, "just welcoming the new folk". He smiled at Leroy's confused expression, "relax, nothing is what it seems here son, so be prepared", his words floated into the perfumed air and the music began.

Nothing could have prepared Leroy for the beauty of this gathering. Herm took his place in the circle opposite the beautiful lady and the gathering closed their eyes. Musical notes drifted from the organ and danced around them. And then, quietly at first, no more than a whisper, an exquisite voice began to intermingle with the dancing musical notes. It was the beautiful lady, singing from her heart, and Daniel, Leroy and Veronica took a seat on the floor, tea in hand, eyes closed and feeling the voice ring through their bodies. The beautiful music continued to dance through them and was almost too much to bear for Leroy who could feel the prick of tears in his eyes. Leroy could see the colours of the music pierce through his eyelids. At first a spattering of yellow with a border of blue, which morphed into yellow with a border of red and then the red devoured the yellow and then disappeared into the black. Leroy could then see flecks of light in the black moving around like cosmic glitter. And then the music seemed to fade away into the colours, dancing in the blackness of his eyes. Following this was a period of complete and utter silence. Leroy kept his eyes closed and wanted to stay like that forever. In the penetrating darkness of his mind, Leroy felt that for the first time he could see.

At length the fluttering thoughts of life began to force his eyelids open and Leroy felt an abrupt panic that the whole gathering was staring at him. But the whole room was silently meditating except for Veronica who was now shyly peaking out of her embarrassing spiritual journey and smiling awkwardly at Leroy. At length the gathering began to wake and started to walk around the room muttering to each other or picking up books from the bookshelves and silently reading cross legged on the floor. The two people who remained the longest in deep meditation was the beautiful lady and Herm who were seated opposite each other. Herm was the first to open his eyes and stared at the lady for a little while before he too got up and walked over to Daniel, Veronica and Leroy who were still huddled together, not entirely comfortably.

"Daniel, why can't you ever relax?" Herm was seated with them in the corner of the basement hall playing chess on an old fashioned looking chess board. Leroy had found an interesting book called 'The political plight of the Gifted' and was reading it intently. Veronica was curled up against the wall in a very deep sleep. "That's the trouble with you 'Pyros', you always seem to be waiting to shoot at something". Herm turned to Leroy and smiled, "So what's your gift then Leroy?". "Teleporting I suppose" answered Leroy shyly, not knowing whether he should refer to him as 'Your Excellency' as the others did. "That's very good" Herm slid his King along the chess board "very good for a sticky wicket". Daniel let out a cry of exasperation, "How about best out of five?" smirked Herm and Daniel crossly began rearranging the chess pieces. Leroy looked across at the beautiful woman, who had been in the grasp of a meditative trance for the best part of an hour. Herm observed Leroy's curious gaze "Her name's Ghazal", said Herm. Leroy felt his cheeks flush crimson and stumbled over his words "Oh, I wasn't looking at her, I was just uh, well I was obviously looking but not in that kind of way, I just, you know", "Relax!" said Herm forcing back a laugh, "I'm just letting you know who she is, she's a very important woman and so you should really meet her when she comes back". Leroy was perplexed by this last part "Sorry, comes back? Comes back from where?". Herm fixed Leroy with his unendingly deep eyes, "Leroy, when most gifted people go into a trance they go into the place just below the exterior, they can feel the blood coursing through their veins, they can feel their heart beating in time with their personally unique song, they can see their soul. But when Ghazal goes to that place she goes much, much further. She goes into her soul, then into her heart and then further still. She can see the entire universe within her and consequently it takes her a great deal more time to navigate through her being. Trust me Leroy, she'll be out for hours. Now do you all want to get something to eat, I'm starving!"

Ghazal was still exploring the realms of her soul while Herm, Leroy, Daniel and Veronica went upstairs to the kitchen at the back of the bookshop. Herm was frying some eggs and Veronica, feeling like a third leg, decided to help out and make the toast. Daniel was moping around the kitchen still sulking about his repeated losses at chess and Leroy was sitting quietly at the kitchen table. "So Herm", Leroy spoke into the air, "What's your gift". Herm chuckled and smiled kindly at Leroy, "My gift is none, Leroy, my gift is simply a tiny amount of knowledge". Daniel finally sat down at the breakfast table as Herm brought over the eggs "Hermes is a walking encyclopedia". "Well, I should be, I've been around for long enough", Herm began to dig into his eggs. "How old are you?", Leroy chomped on his toast and stared at Herm's flawlessly wrinkle free face and athletic body, trying to place his age. Herm looked up and smiled cheekily "I'm 370 years old". Veronica let out a cry of laughter while Leroy let out a subdued chortle "Come on! Seriously, how old are you?". Herm gazed into Leroy's eyes, and as Leroy stared back he could see words, numbers, algebra and art running behind his eye sockets. Herm smiled, "I have seen many things in my life, empires built and overthrown, war, famine, and yet it is only knowledge that I have kept within me. I have studied all Leroy, and yet I know nothing, I am ignorant of the ways of the world"

"Now that's not exactly true Hermes", said a new voice. Leroy swung around and looked towards the kitchen door where Ghazal was standing in nonchalant style. "Ghazal! Come and have something to eat, you must be exhausted", Ghazal walked over and sat in the only empty seat next to Leroy, and as she sat down Leroy felt as though he couldn't breath and shifted uncomfortably in his chair. "Thanks Hermes, but I'm not hungry, my journey kind of makes me forget about food." She smiled and turned to look at Leroy, her eyes penetrating deep into his being, "So are you a gifted too?", "Uh, yes" stammered Leroy with a mouthful of egg spraying out a little, "I'm a, uh, a teleporter". "That's nice" Ghazal smiled sweetly at Leroy making his heart skip a beat, "being able to leave a bad situation is a very useful gift" she gazed out of the window with a far off look in her eyes and Leroy noticed Herm had an almost imperceptible look of concern on his face.

Seated there at the breakfast table Leroy felt a profound sense of awe in Ghazal's presence. He did not feel that she was his equal but rather that she was like a famous celebrity. As she sat there and gazed serenely out of the window he felt in the presence of an almost higher power. He noted Veronica's slightly jealous eyes as she looked down, her eyebrows furrowed with the appearance of concentration as she casually perused the book in front of her, and Leroy realised that he felt nothing but love for her. With Ghazal it was a different kind of love, a pure admiration which made him want to be a better man and Leroy felt utterly at peace.

"Is everything ok?" Ghazal's sweet voice cajoled Leroy from his reverie. "Oh yes, sorry, I was just thinking about something!" spluttered Leroy shattering the silence with his own awkward voice. "Well that's always a good thing, thinking about something is always better than not", chirped Herm, "I for example was thinking how it's been such a long time before I had porridge. I remember eating a Chinese porridge not so long ago made with rice, ginger and soy sauce, and as I recall it was a terrible faux pas on my part to add honey to it!" Veronica chuckled and contemplatively ran her fingers over the pages of the book in front of her, returning Leroy's smile and heavenwards look of teenage sarcasm.

Suddenly there was a loud banging on the door and they heard a high whiny laugh outside the front door. "Here little piggies! Come out, come out wherever you are!"

"Vermeer!" hissed Daniel as he clenched his fists in subconscious anticipation. "How did they know we were here?" cried out Veronica, eyes widened in fear.

Herm looked at them with a confused expression, "Wait, what do you mean? Why are they looking for *you*?" Daniel started shuffling guiltily, prepared for the ultimate admonishment, "that was … erm … kind of down to me", Herm's eyes were fixed on Daniel with a look of deep foreboding "And why would that be Dan?". "Well, I told Ninety Nine that Leroy was the Hundredth Soul. I didn't know what else to do, it was to protect …", Daniel had seemingly reverted to the frightened child that Leroy remembered from so long ago. They heard the commotion was getting louder outside the front door, but Herm's face was calm "Well, for future reference, perhaps you shouldn't bring a target to a large gathering of people, putting everyone in danger."

There was a loud crack on the front door and Leroy and Daniel ran upstairs to see what was happening outside. Looking through the window they saw three burly men with large axes laughing as the axe crashed down upon the door. Standing beside them was a tall gaunt gentleman with fierce eyes and a beak like nose. Leroy and Daniel ran back to the kitchen where Herm was protectively putting a large grey duffle coat around Ghazal's shoulders covering her thin dress, his eyes fixed on Leroy "You're going to have to help us get out of here". All looked expectedly at Leroy as he shifted uncomfortably. "But I need to … I mean … I don't know where" there was a loud crash and the horrible sound of splintering wood. "Anywhere!" screamed Daniel, "You have to do it now! Quick everyone, hold on to him. Leroy now!". Leroy closed his eyes and tried to think of a place "Where should I go?" he shouted into the darkness, "I can't think of anywhere!". "Home, no they'll be there" Veronica thought out loud with surprising calm in light of the ever nearing laughter and smashing furniture, "Hyde Park, Bucks House, St Paul's Cathedral!".

Suddenly there was a flash and when Leroy opened his eyes he was standing before a cross in the crypt of St Paul's Cathedral. "Well", mused Herm, "that was relatively painless, good job Captain." Leroy went over and collapsed on a pew and tried to let the exhaustion of the teleport pass over him. He now realised that teleporting himself was not unduly difficult, however, transporting a party of five severely depleted his energy resources. Leroy's eyelids began to close and as they did he could make out the worried expression of Veronica as she hurried towards him. Then only darkness.

Leroy awoke to find the four of them seated on the chairs in the crypt chapel in serious conference. The chairs had been moved into a circle and all had sober looks on their faces "This is an extremely dangerous situation for us, Leroy needs to be moved elsewhere, they cannot be together." Herm acknowledged Leroy's nearing presence with a sombre nod. "Look" Leroy's voice pierced the silence, "I think it would be best for me to teleport to some far off land, and for nobody to know where I am, that way you could all be safe." "You can't, and besides that won't work Leroy" Veronica's voice was quaking slightly with passion. Leroy looked away from her to the other three "I've made the decision. Since I'm the Hundredth Soul I can make the decision. It's my call entirely". Herm looked puzzled, "I beg your pardon? Has Daniel not explained everything to you?" he shot Daniel a disapproving look, "Leroy, you're not the Hundredth Soul, Ghazal is." Ghazal smiled shyly, "Daniel only told Ninety Nine that you were the Hundredth Soul so that it would take some heat off Ghazal whilst she was my student. It was important to protect her from all the outside forces and assassination attempts in order to help her with her gift, Leroy" he noted the disappointment in Leroy's face "your actions are helping to save all Gifted people, you have done so much for all of us for which we are all eternally grateful."

Leroy sat on the pew, mortified. He had been so utterly convinced that he was special, that he had something to give the world. Now it was all over and he was back to being a nobody again with nothing to offer Veronica; only a free flight but no airmiles. He smiled sadly to himself and looked over at Veronica who was running her fingers over the plaque belonging to William Blake. He decided that he may not be a Great Soul but he could still win her affections and he bravely walked over to her. "Do you like poetry?" said Leroy rather loudly, he was aware that the other three who were seated at the pews could hear his every word. "Well, to be honest, not really" Veronica smiled at Leroy, "it's just a load of words and I'm not great at those" Leroy smiled inside "so you're just like a bloke then", he realised what he had just said and spluttered "oh no wait, sorry, I didn't mean that you're like a man, I just meant that .. uh …well". Daniel casually walked past "Smooth!" he muttered sarcastically. Veronica giggled, "relax, Leroy, I know what you meant" she charmingly fluffed her thick blonde hair, through which Leroy could imagine running his hands.

Suddenly there was a loud scream of frustration "It's not working Herm, I can feel it all falling away!" Ghazal was standing and pacing up and down the chapel and Herm had a worried look on his face "Look just keep at it, you've come so far in your training". Ghazal crumpled into her chair and gazed thoughtfully at the cross. Leroy and Veronica exchanged worried looks.

Perhaps cabin fever was beginning to ensue, there was an uncomfortable atmosphere in the crypt's dense air and all five of them could feel it. Daniel, Leroy and Veronica waited. And waited. They talked or paced up and down the crypt. Sometimes they would read the memorial plaques, but often they would sit on the plaques staring into space. All the while Herm and Ghazal were engaged in quietly intense debate. Ghazal was becoming less demure and serene and increasingly panicked and tense. At length they regrouped into their chairs and an icy quiet filled the air. "So" Leroy said unnaturally loudly cutting into the calm, he desperately wanted to recover some dignity having fainted earlier, "What is your gift then Ghazal?". She looked up at him suddenly, eyes fiery and intense, "It's not so much a gift as a curse". Herm was looking anxiously at Ghazal and, turning to Leroy, explained "Leroy, Ghazal has a remarkable power, one so remarkable that she must not under any circumstances use it."

"But", Leroy felt embarrassed to have caused this further tension, "that doesn't make any sense". "Yeah", chimed in Veronica, eyes wide with interest, "What exactly is your power?"

Ghazal seemed to have grown taller, her fiery orange eyes were now locked on Leroy and Veronica. "I control atoms, and that is all". "That's enough of this now" said Herm, "let's talk about something else". They sat in silence, Ghazal was staring at Leroy's perturbed expression. "You really want to know?" she challenged, they both nodded tentatively, aware of Herm's reproving look, "fine!". Ghazal shot Herm a look of triumph as his face turned hauntingly troubled. "I told you", Ghazal said to Herm as he grabbed her arm to stop her, "I cannot change anything Herm, I told you! And now I have returned to the place where I was born all those years ago. My sanctuary, where I am powerful, where nothing can stop me. I told you Hermes, Oh Thoth, Ukhnukh, Idris, son of Zeus, you should have known better! Maybe now the time has come for it all to end so that I may be reborn. I will give you a head start Hermes, one minute for each century you claim to have been through." "Ghazal!" Hermes cried out imploringly, Daniel rose from his seat, eyes filled with terror. "Stop it now, go back! You can go back!", Hermes was gripping hard onto Ghazal's arm. "I can't go back. It has to happen this way", she withdrew her arm from Hermes and floated away, eyes wild, towards Lord Nelson's Chamber.

Herm turned to the three of them, his face drained of blood and looking every day of his three hundred years "Run" he said quietly and Leroy, Daniel and Veronica looked at each other uneasily, "Run!" he screamed, "Get out! We have to get out of here right now". Daniel turned to Leroy with a horrified look on his face "We have to run Leroy, none of our powers will work here, only hers!" Leroy felt sick with panic and before he could think of what to do all four were running out of the crypt. They ran quickly down the pale white corridors, past the dim lamps on the walls, Hermes was shouting "quick, we have to get out! Get to the exit". They pushed the grand door which was slightly ajar and they could see the famous scene of candles, ornate décor and imposing statues. They ran down the side aisle and tried the door, which was locked firmly shut. "Quick let's get to the front door it might be open", they raced to the front but the front doors were also locked. Hermes looked down resignedly and Daniel kicked the leaflet shelf so papers flew out in anarchic style, "It's too late, we can't get out!".

Time began to pass in slow motion, Leroy closed his eyes. He could remember the last time he had come to the cathedral as a boy. How he had run around the aisles mesmerised by the sombre beauty of the place and how he had pressed his hand against the dome in the stone gallery and run around, not at all phased by the amount of stairs. A myriad of memories ran through his mind when suddenly there was a flash. Leroy opened his eyes and saw all four of them balancing on top of the dome. They all immediately sat down and grabbed the cold stone for balance to prevent them from falling. Daniel and Hermes were staring at Leroy in disbelief, "How did you do that?" cried Hermes. "I don't know!" Leroy couldn't understand what had just happened.

Suddenly there was a large explosion and St Paul's Cathedral's dome shot up a few metres, with the four of them holding on for dear life. They looked down and the cathedral was slowly disintegrating into millions of tiny particles which were dancing around in the air. The dome was floating in the air and then came crashing down onto the floor, shattering into pieces. Then the roar of the crashing abated and the cool wind began to weave between the sharp pieces, whistling between the spaces. The haunting melody of destruction playing loudly around the place of this historical monument, which was now crushed into oblivion.

After a while the rubble began to move slightly and Leroy's aching body crawled out to the sound of police sirens. He carefully walked over the debris, trying to navigate with a sharp ringing in his ears, and then collapsed onto the cold hard ground. In the midst of the ringing he heard the screech of rubber, doors slamming and, at length, he heard footsteps running towards him. He found Daniel seated on the boot of a police car with his arm in a sling. Herm was leaning against the car door nursing some bruises. "Are you ok?", Leroy was so pleased to see them his voice was croaking slightly with emotion, "I've been better" replied Herm. Suddenly Leroy had a painful snap of realisation as he saw the haunted look on Daniel's face "Veronica?", Daniel sadly looked away from Leroy's pleading face, Leroy followed Daniel's gaze to see a stretcher next to the ambulance in which lay a slight body covered by rough cloth. Leroy could hear Herm's gentle voice and the quiet sonata of condolences around him but he was not listening. He stood motionless as he was bandaged around the head and was expressionless as he was placed in a stretcher. His whole world made and destroyed in a few days, a few bizarre moments. Never could he go back to how things were before, and why would he want to anyway.

Daniel was muttering something about staying with Herm and guarding Leroy in hospital whilst he was under observation, "Shouldn't be more than a few weeks". Words were floating around before him and all he could think of was Veronica. How he had failed her. From the corner of his eye he noticed that Herm was staring at him strangely. All of a sudden Hermes walked towards Leroy and without warning reached for his right hand and held it up to reveal the black pyramid shaped mark. Herm studied him as Daniel kept repeating that everything would be alright and that he would call his parents. Eventually Daniel and Hermes left Leroy, with Hermes giving Leroy one last curious glance as they walked away into the distance.

Leroy turned his head to the remains of the Cathedral as the nurses began to lift him onto the ambulance. Seeing the fragments of the once grand structure tore at his heart. The particles would not settle and in the twilight seemed to form a supernatural mist through which suddenly he could see the outline of a figure. He strained his eyes and could see Ghazal's faintly serene and beautiful face with tears streaming from her eyes. As he was being led into the ambulance he called out weakly to the pure light in her eyes but she disappeared into the mist. And then.

And then there was only dust.

To be continued

Mutiny on the Grampus

Had the time passed so slowly? Now I am old and there is no respite from the unmerciful ravages of time. If only I could combust in a flash rather than wither and slowly sink into the ground. But there is a long time before that, an eternity indeed.

And what of my past, you ask. I see your curious face yet I do not respond. I do not want to answer that, not yet. I still need to recover. You persist and I would like you to stop writing and put the papers back inside your pristine briefcase. But you don't, and keep writing with long purposeful strokes of your pen. Your forehead is furrowed in deep concentration and your eyes occasionally fix me with a look of pity. I am old, yes, but I can see that look and I am not dead, not yet.

You visit me everyday and sit by my bed. Sometimes you just watch me as I gaze up at the pure white ceiling. Sometimes you write fiercely into your notepad or leaf through the pages in your file. Often you tell me I should talk but I do not want to. What I want to do is run the length of the corridor outside my room and bang on the doors of my fellow inmates, singing wildly. But alas my legs are weak and my brittle bones would crush onto the floor. Yet in my dreams, when your pen is not scribbling to fill the silences, I run for miles. I run down the streets of Nantucket where I grew up. I run to the door of my sweetheart and watch her gazing out of the upstairs window, that is until her father sees me and chases me away. I run to the church late on my wedding day and then run to the hospital to greet my new born son. I run away from those who love me. No, enough of that, my eyes feel wet. I can now see your wide eyes staring at me in disbelief, your pen suspended in midair. I say aloud that whatever little faith I had tells me that I am nearly dead and before I go I have something to say. You slowly drop pen to paper so I may begin my tale.

...

Date: 20 November 1870
Report of Inmate 325

I must confess this is a rather curious case. Inmate 325 is now 72 years old and of very poor health. I have been observing him

for some 9 months now and he displays no more responsiveness than a comatose patient. I have been informed by my predecessor that he is capable of speech and his hearing is not impaired, however, in my 9 months of observation he has not said a word or even acknowledged my presence. All I have seen is him laying horizontally on his bed either staring up at the ceiling or dully ahead when propped up for washing. I had nearly lost all hope that I would make any progress with Inmate 325, when today, quite unexpectedly, I had an incredible breakthrough. I was flicking through my file looking for something I could say to invoke some sort of response. I had not yet said a word all morning and was quietly sipping my coffee in what had now become a daily routine. I then had an uncanny feeling that I was being observed, yet thought it impossible since Inmate 325 had not even acknowledged my existence. I was being urged by some sixth sense and a prickle shot down the back of my neck prompting me to look up, and upon looking up I saw a most extraordinary sight. Inmate 325's head was inclined towards me and his deep eyes were staring at my face. I nearly fell off my chair in shock! I immediately looked away, not able to handle his penetrating stare but when I slowly turned my head back I saw tears dripping from his eyes and I was strangely comforted into being a doctor again. When he spoke his voice croaked and splintered into the dense silence which had devoured the atmosphere these past nine months.

This report shall be a record of the story related to me by Inmate 325. I have done my best for my report to be as accurate a reflection as possible of the words used by Inmate 325, however, in some parts I have had to explain what was said through my own notes where details have become hazy or when Inmate 325 has become evasive or otherwise reverted back to silence. And thus, here begins the story of Captain Barnard.

...

I was 21 when I proposed to my wife, Evelyn. Young and childlike, I imagined that my love for her could withstand anything. I remember strolling along the roads of my childhood, spring in my step, song in my heart, thinking about my love. It was foolish obsession I now know. When I proposed to her I meant it with all my heart, yet as preparation for the wedding began I grew increasingly distant and withdrawn, as if life was somehow passing me by.

The wedding took place on a bitter cold December day. I awoke with a deep ache in my head and my entire body felt as though it had frozen solid beneath my paper thin blanket. I had a deep sense of foreboding as I lay there, still and frozen, awaiting some unknown doom. At length I managed to rise and slowly walked to my window where before me was the most beautiful scene I had ever beheld. Beneath the orange glow of the morning sun was an expanse of fields blanketed with pure white snow. A winter wonderland which propelled me back to my childhood. The lake at the front of my house had frozen over and the ice shimmered in the light of the sun. I gazed ahead at this beauty, feeling that this scene before me was more magical than the vows I was due to take, and a sharp pain stabbed at my heart. I had only ever heard of the paradox of happiness and sadness entwined in each other's arms like lovers, yet until then I had never felt its existence. However, as I gazed ahead with the salty tears gushing down my icy cheeks I felt it clearly and it was in that moment that I became a man, leaving the child I once was running behind me in the snow. His footsteps remain imprinted forever like some heartbreaking emblem of past happiness.

I walked down the aisle to my new life and immediately after returning from our honeymoon I threw myself into my work. I worked hard and became a proficient whaleman and Evelyn became the perfect housewife. What still amazes me is how quickly we fitted into our respective roles, forever playing house together and trying to forget the piercing boredom of the monotony of married life. She was bored too, I could sense, and desperately wanted some distraction to give her life meaning. So more than two years later I became Captain of my first ship, the Ivy, and Evelyn had given birth to our first and only son, Augustus. I was never there at the beginning with our son, and not really there at the end.

At the time she went into labour I was sailing gleefully among the waves, riding towards my destiny. As it transpired, my destiny lay waiting for me in a brothel in Nantucket. I had arrived early from my voyage and as I bid farewell to my companions my heavy feet shuffled along the road to my heavily pregnant wife but each step I took brought me closer to panic with heart wrenching speed and eventually I found myself turning on my heels and bounding across the other side of town. What I was hoping to find was simply a sanctuary, a box in which I could lock myself away from false reality, away from frightening responsibility.

NB: Inmate 325 is silent for a long while. I tried to coax him back to telling his story but he did not speak until some time had passed by.

What I found instead was Kate, standing by a tall lamppost watching me walk towards her with my eyes vacant. I felt the sting of tears running down my cheeks as I realised that nothing would ever be the same. I remember running down the streets to Evelyn the next day and seeing her lying there in the hospital bed, tears in her eyes holding her new life. That day I hovered in the background and did so for the next 16 years like a ghost. The only time I felt alive was when I was standing proudly at the helm of the Ivy, the clammy breeze rustling through my hair and the sound of my lads' footsteps running along the deck towards the starboard as they heaved the carcass of a large whale on board.

When Augustus was 16 his mother died from tuberculosis and it then fell on me to be responsible for this young stranger. It was the end of the freedom I had childishly clung onto for so many years although I believe that I took to this new role of father very well. Having said that, I realise that the hard part was over and young Augustus was a fully functioning little man whose only ambition, it seemed, was to be like me in every way. I let him wear my clothes and smoke my pipe and eventually I decided to take him sailing on the Ivy, now one of the best whaling ships in the south. I taught him how to sail, how to be a whaleman and within a year he became a fine member of the crew.

NB: The section on his son and his adultery took quite some time to confirm since he had decided to tell me without any detail. It is only with my pressing him that he described his child's birth after his deed. I am slightly disturbed by his confession of adultery since there are clearly links between sexual deviance

and amorality in a patient's other conduct. I would advise that we continue to observe Inmate 325 for any other signs of perversion.

One fine summer morning my crew set sail on board the Ivy heading for waters north. I had undertaken very little planning for this expedition, however with each day moored on land I was becoming increasingly restless. Land did not much suit me anymore and I was therefore content to set sail as soon as practicable. So I hustled up my crew and we set sail, with me at the wheel of the Ivy; a picture of contentment. My crew consisted of sailors I had known for years and who were extremely proficient in their own drunken ways. Dirk Peters was by far the most experienced mate of the bunch and I was rather surprised that he had not made first mate or captain. He did however lack ambition and was content to drink himself into a stupor, sleep on deck and lend the occasional hand to the crew. Richard Parker, on the other hand, was an experienced harpooner and wanted all the crew to know it, especially me. He was a very hard worker and I felt content that the Ivy was safe in his and Dirk's hands. Another to whom I was absolutely reliant upon was the services of our black cook, I think his name was John, who was a whaleman more and cook less. He would make sure that the boys were fed and would lend a hand wherever necessary to steer the Ivy straight and true towards our destination as well as hauling up the whales we caught.

The person, however, who I felt most comfortable with was my first mate and friend, Robert, who had served me these past ten years. There was none other in whom I could place my absolute trust, not even my own flesh was as close to me.

NB: Inmate 325 refused to elaborate on the circumstances of meeting Robert and anything else about their friendship.

And so the Ivy sailed on, with the mates singing songs and sipping rum, our façade of normal living left behind and caged in our strong walled houses. The cook brought his two brothers to help and whilst I was initially hesitant to let all three of them on board it soon became clear that they were invaluable to the crew and I do not know what I would have done without them. They fed the crew, they sailed the ship and they mended anything that needed mending, including our spirits. Yes, the Ivy was a happy ship and, oh, that it would have continued thus.

One morning around 6 months in we sailed across the north seas on the lookout for a huge 'right' whale to make our voyage a success. One of the mates had seen it swim by the ship and raised the alarm. We anchored the Ivy and quickly readied the whale boats to follow behind the monstrous whale. Three whaleboats were due to sail out to anchor at various points in prediction of the course of the right whale. Dirk, Augustus and two other whalemen went into one boat with Augustus volunteering to be the harpooner. I was in another boat with Robert, closer to the Whaleship so that I could keep an eye on the rest of the crew. We waited in the stillness of the salty air for some movement beneath the opaque water. The rest of the crew waited patiently on the Ivy, eyes fixed on the water below. Eventually there was a rustle in the water and the monstrous dark blue outline passed beneath. One of the mates began to stomp fairly quietly on the deck in what had become their secret code, which was heard by Robert who nodded in the direction of the other whaleboat and Augustus moved to the edge of his whale boat, arms outstretched in anticipation.

I saw Augustus' steely eyes fixed on the water in the direction of the whaleship where the whale had just passed by. I knew then that Augustus was a naturally gifted whaleman, and why wouldn't he be, he was my son. For many years before I had met his mother I had accompanied my father on whaleships and learnt my trade with a keenness and dedication that my friends, who were more accustomed to land, could not quite comprehend. And there he was now, eyes fixed on his target, mind in complete focus and, suddenly, Augustus' arms came down with a powerful force and stabbed two irons into the whale's body. Following this the rest of the crew tied the lines to keep the whale close to the boat. Upon the irons piercing into its thick wet armoury the whale heaved forward in pain and the whalemen held fast onto the boat as the whale pulled them forward through the sea.

The whale sped on dragging the whaleboat with Augustus holding on tight for his life. These 'Nantucket sleigh rides', as they were colloquially known would typically last for around one to three hours and would often result in the death of some of the whalemen who would fall overboard and not be rescued in time. After a while it transpired that the whale was not yet mortally wounded as Augustus had missed its vital organs entirely. So Augustus jabbed two more irons into the whale in motion but this only spurred the whale to go faster. We stood on deck watching the hideously comical sight of the mammoth beast dragging the boat back and forth, praying that the whale would tire so that Augustus could stab it again.

After an hour or so the whale tired and stopped a short distance from the whaleship. Augustus picked up two further irons and held them up in the air, however, upon doing so the whale suddenly jerked forward causing Augustus to trip over himself thereby losing his grip on the irons. Augustus scrabbled to the side of the boat and watched the irons sink into the cold water and before he could decide what to do next the whale was speeding ahead. In spite of the horror that was unfolding before us and the potential consequences, we stood there with vacant grins on our faces watching this entirely usual scene. Until.

"Oh my God!", we cried out as we awoke from our dull stupor, "they're coming towards us!". Having been spectators thus far watching the Nantucket sleigh ride we were now part of the show. We started running in a blind panic and whilst I tried to shout down the ensuing terror on the whaleship I could not quell it. Before I could think of what to do I heard the sickening sound of crushing wood. Dirk frantically began to cut the line from the boat and allowed the whale to swim away with undisguised nonchalance whilst our noises of dread drowned the sea air. The whalemen jumped overboard to avoid the splintering wood and swam towards us as we safely sat watching in our whale boats. And there, huddled shivering together, we watched the Ivy sink before our eyes in a sad descent into the deep.

After our rescue I stayed at home floundering in a melancholic state. My beard grew long, my eyes were full of manic despair and I neither washed nor ate to the disgust of Augustus, whom I largely ignored. After 6 months of wallowing in my failure in a condition of abject poverty I decided to leave the house and as fate would have it I bought a new whaleship that very day. I was convinced that it was my destiny to now sail this new ship, the Grampus, to glory so I sold Evelyn's jewellery to purchase it. I could tell from Augustus' eyes that this was a horrid deed, and I confess that I cannot recall that I saw any unforced tenderness from his eyes after I had committed it. Luckily Augustus was soon distracted when I told him that he would be joining me on a whaling voyage soon, and we began readying the ship. Due to the shortage of funds I was forced to let some of my whalemen go so I brought the cook with me but decided to pay him a lower wage and to let his brothers go. As I told him this I noticed a bitter smile from him and he simply stated that it was all he could expect from me. I, of course, agreed with him, since clearly I had to give priority to the other whalemen despite my fondness for him and his brothers.

As preparations for our voyage were underway I noticed a somewhat distracted manner in Augustus. He would go for long periods in complete silence and not acknowledge my existence, and when he did talk to me it was only to badger me to take his 16 year old friend, Arthur Pym, with us on the voyage. I expressly forbid this as I did not want another novice on the next voyage since I did not want anything to go wrong. I could not help blaming Augustus for the sinking of the Ivy, and although I did not tell him so I could see that he also understood this to be the case. I could see the look of disappointment on his face and felt rather guilty so, at the moment we were due to set sail, I gave him permission to run and get Arthur, though surprisingly he refused!

And then we set off, bound for the south seas. After a couple of days I noticed that Augustus was acting suspiciously. He had inexplicably brought Arthur's dog onto the ship, for which I lost my temper with him. Then I noticed he was sneaking away with food at various times and I came to the conclusion that he had brought Arthur as a stowaway on board and secreted him on some part of the ship, despite my specific instructions not to allow him on board. I did not want to mention my suspicions since I wanted Augustus to confess himself so I decided to wait a little while before saying anything. However, shortly after we had set off a horrifying course of events began to unfold which to this day sends chills down my spine.

I awoke one morning to the sound of a great ruckus and, eyes squinting in the morning light, I walked over to the deck buttoning up my shirt. I saw the cook towering over Robert with his cutlass curved around Robert's neck. Dirk was shouting that there did not have to be any blood, and a wild eyed Richard Parker was squaring up to my cousin, Blake. Robert saw me coming towards them and screamed

"Captain, it's a mutiny! They're all in on it!" and I was grabbed from behind and brought down to the floor.

I heard the slow footsteps of the cook's hard boots on the deck, every step pounding through my body. He grabbed my hair with his blistered hands and drew my face towards him. I saw his cold face break out into a callous smile, "Come on Captain, surely you couldn't expect anything more!". "Father!", I heard Augustus running towards me but he was soon grappled to the floor "It's ok son, don't worry!" I shouted through the tumult. I felt the cook's cutlass pressed against my throat, "Now now Captain, do you really want to lie to the boy?" his smile widened, "Put him on the boat!" The sailors cheered and sang as they hauled me into the whaleboat with Robert. Richard grasped Blake's arm and threw him into the boat with me, with Blake's fervent protestations falling on deaf ears. Andrew, a shy young boy who was largely an outcast in the midst of the drunken sailors was also thrown in with us. Some sailors reached for Augustus who was looking back towards some part of the ship in deep concern. The cook noticed this and pulled him back saying that he was to stay on the Grampus and threw him back onto the floor while the crewmen hurriedly cut our boat's rope in a frenzy. As we drifted away I saw Augustus run towards us with tears streaming down his face. Upon hearing one of the drunken sailors coming towards him I watched as he hid away behind a large fishing net.

And thus we were cast away into the blue, completely at the mercy of the tempestuous seas. We sat huddled together in the crisp evening air. I was shivering in my morning shirt bizarrely regretting the fact that I had not been better prepared for the sudden unexpected mutiny. Blake was furiously rocking back and forth longingly staring back in the direction of the whaleship and Robert draped one side of his coat around my shoulders as I leaned into his torso like a frightened child. With my head pressed against Robert's chest I looked over at Andrew with immense curiosity. He sat there in the stillness of the night air staring up at the stars with childlike dreaminess that demonstrated his 16 years of age. I confess I was suspicious of him from the start. He was suggested to me by Robert who told me he was brought to him by a priest. Robert explained how Andrew had come to him with pleading eyes and empty pockets, which I could tell had tugged at Robert's heart strings. And whilst I allowed him to join us I was still suspicious of him since he had a thoughtful academic look about him which did not fit the profile of a whaleman.

I saw Blake fingering the few food provisions and bottles of water that had been tossed in with us. Blake had a naturally cheery disposition and was popular with the crew. I felt content that Blake and Robert were in the boat with me but I felt a pinch in my heart when I thought about Augustus. Was he safe? A tear rolled down my cheek and I turned my head into Robert's chest and let the stream of sadness flow out without any inhibition. Robert patted my back and after a while all was silent again but entirely awkward between us.

As some time had passed from our horrendous casting off, Blake was able to regain some modicum of composure and began to rally the three of us to believe that salvation would come. It was of course only a couple of days since we had set off from shore and we hoped that our guardian angels would guide our boat back so we could envelop ourselves into the warm bosom of the earth. Alas the mutineers left us stranded with no compass so we studied the fall of the sun and tried to fix our eyes on a spot in the unending ocean, but our tired malnourished minds could not follow our course in the blackness of the night.

After a while our eyes began to adjust and we could faintly made out each other's faces reflected in the moonlight. Blake began to tell joyful stories of his youth but we could see the sadness in his eyes as he recalled his glorious past and after a while we were choking on the hopelessness of our situation and turning to the only force that could help our weak bodies and weaker souls. Robert recited the Lord's prayer with a sombre voice but we could hear the deafening banging notes of desperation in the silences between each word. And as for Andrew, he did not say a word.

I realised as I sat there in the freezing night air that hours had passed and I had not made a sound except for the chatter of my teeth and the loud grumbling of my stomach. I noticed that Robert's eyes would every so often look down at me, as if to make sure I was still alive. I was living, yes, but not alive. My whole being had frozen solid. The sharp pain of the cold breeze was jabbing into my flesh and slowly absorbing into my brittle bones. I lay still as if any movement could result in a thunderous symphony of cracks and my body would be split into a thousand pieces. Even my mind had frozen. No thoughts had entered my tired brain as it dully observed this scene of despair. I felt that if a thought found its way through this icicle filled cave where my brain sat there would be a deafening sound of crashing ice and then my mind would be left to melt in the freezing water. As this realisation hit me I awoke from my vacant trance. As I felt Robert's eyes on me again and listened to Blake's monologue my thoughts came creeping back. And that was when a thousand tears began to flow from my eyes again, without warning. What sort of Captain, nay, what sort of man am I? I lacked the calm meditative nature of Andrew, the parental kindness of Robert or the leadership in the face of adversity displayed by Blake. I simply sat with my crew in a limp redundant mess. I pulled away from Robert to face the sea and let my tears fall away into the water so that my shame could swim away from me. Staring at the black twilight sky I saw images of the events which had unfolded playing out like a show just for me. Had I become delirious, or was this vision really before me? The lines between delirium and reality had now blurred so irretrievably in my misery. There was a gradual heaviness on my eyelids and soon I was trapped in my own black sky until morning suddenly ripped open the skies with light.

As we slowly sipped some bottled water that remained we collectively had a sense of deep foreboding in sharp contrast to the bright morning sky that was smiling at us. Though we had survived yet another night, the difficulty of our survival only seemed to compound our fear that we would not survive another. We watched birds circling overhead in unabashed joy yet for us the hunger and hopelessness intensified.

"So there I was, looking for a book to give to her but quite unable to find anything which would suit her disposition" Blake was recounting one of his many romantic tales, "… and quite unable to find any book that would represent my deep love for her. But it was a deep love, let me tell you that and if I were still in Nantucket I would be …". Blake looked at the boat floor wistfully.

"And what about you? Have you ever experienced love?" I asked in a sudden bolt out of the blue. Robert and Blake looked pensively at each other, "Do you mean me?" Robert asked.

"I think he means me" replied a quite voice and Andrew returned my deep stare with a shy smile, "No Captain, I have never experienced love".

"Well", I began to talk loudly and felt a bolt of exhilaration rush down my spine, "that's clearly a lie, isn't it. You have clearly experienced some kind of love, be it from your parents, siblings or even friends". I smiled at Robert who nervously looked at Andrew with parental concern. "You know Andrew, the fact that this is the first thing you have said to me since you arrived on our voyage, since our initial passing greeting, makes me wonder about you."

Andrew had fixed me with a calm stare looking remarkably poised for a boy of his age. Blake seemed to be enjoying this new development in the boat since it gave him respite from his self allocated entertaining duties. Robert, sensing my wretched tone of bitterness, was desperate to change the subject. But no, I would not let him, I could feel the hunger rising within me and I needed a target.

"Yes, it really makes me wonder, Andrew. I know all my whalemen, I know who they are, I know their families. I know what makes them tick, what doesn't. And throughout this voyage I have observed you. Maybe on some subconscious level at first, and more intensely these last days, and I have deduced something very disturbing about you. You are not a whaleman."

There was a tentative pause as we waited for the boat to capsize and drown this new awkwardness.

"It wasn't a lie", Andrew replied assertively.

"I think I know what a whaleman is, since I have..." I began, incensed at the boy's flagrant insubordination, "No, you don't know what I mean" Andrew cut me short, "I have never known love, Captain, just as you have never loved land"

"Why," I exclaimed "the utter impertinence of this young scamp, who was not so long ago still crying in his mother's bosom" Robert tried to calm the ensuing tension but I was bursting with hysterical excitement, which was soothing my aching body like a drug.

"Just look at the facts Andrew. You do not drink with my other whalemen, you displayed no more than a passing interest in the workings of a whaleship and when you arrived I noticed you carrying a leather pouch which you have since kept on your person at all times". "That's right" chimed in Blake, "a most peculiar thing, I noticed that too but didn't draw attention to it. He still has it now. What's in the pouch Andrew?" Blake demanded.

"I'll tell you!" I was in full swing "I noticed that while the other men were singing merrily, young Andrew had slipped into a quiet corner and removed from the pouch a book. A book!"

"What a queer thing to bring on a whaleship" now even Robert was amazed "Why did you bring a book onto a whaleship Andrew?"

All three of us had now assumed the roles of interrogators and had fixed Andrew with expectant stares waiting for our subject to wilt under our cross examination. However, I had the sickening supposition in the depths of my overexcited brain that no matter what answer he gave, it would be the wrong one. I felt powerful again and did not want to lose it in the salty streams of my choking heart.

"So I could write" came Andrew's surprisingly calm reply.

"Write!" exclaimed Blake, "you can write? What in God's holy name would you ever need to write about?"

"My journey" Andrew was now looking gravely at the floor.

"Journey?" Blake spat out his words as if they tasted of rotten food.

"More importantly," I said "why are you here on a whaleship voyage in the midst of sodden clothes and bitter sweet drink if you are literate?" I sat shell shocked looking at Andrew's solemn figure with his angelic grace and slightly quivering lips. Then I leaned in slightly, my eyes stabbing into him with cold fury, "Who are you?"

Andrew looked directly at me as if wanting to say something but then looked down. "It was you wasn't it?" I said finally through gritted teeth. I wanted to leap over and completely destroy his deceitful look of piety, "*You* started the mutiny, *you* caused this!"

Andrew did not respond but had a pained expression on his face. "Yes" said Blake excitedly, "I'm sure it was him. I mean look at him, he's not even denying it"

More silence.

"Why did you do it?" I let out an exasperated cry, "Now wait a minute" said Robert "I don't think he could have...."

"WHY?" I screamed, feeling the madness rise within me. Andrew was now looking at me with wide eyes, a scared and confused young boy. There was then a long awkward silence as we each attempted to regain some composure.

"You know", said Blake quietly, "you caused this ... so you must pay for it" Robert's shaking voice tried to rise above the poisonous atmosphere, "I think we might be heading west and need to turn. I'm pretty positive that shore is that way".

"There is no shore" I muttered almost inaudibly, "There is no rescue, no hope, just our bodies left to decay. We have no more provisions Robert, how long do you think we will last. We have nothing, we might as well be chewing on our own hands".

"That sounds like a good idea" Blake was speaking quietly and looking at Andrew with an almost animalistic hunger. "We won't make another night, Captain, we only have one option" he paused and studied my complicit expression "to pick out one of us to eat. That is the only way, the only way that some of us will survive, if we don't we are all certain to die."

"No!" screamed Robert slightly hysterically "No!"

"It's the only way" Blake pleaded "Robert you know that it's the only way. Look, we'll make it painless, it's for the greater good. We'll draw straws."

"There's no need" I was now laughing with fanatical glee, "no need to draw for we know who it will be", I was staring at Andrew's frightened face. Every ounce of my being wanted to destroy him, to obliterate the cause of my misery. It was difficult to know which was stronger, my hunger for flesh or destruction. I had a wide fixed grin and manic look in my eyes and I could not hear Robert's voice of reason. I lunged onto Andrew with surprising speed and clamped my hands around his scrawny neck. He was screaming "Let me go!", "Please!", and then screamed for his father before his eyes almost popped out of their sockets and then he remained there in my hands, limp and cold.

It was Blake who Robert ordered, with bitter anger, to cut up the first pieces of meat. He broke the wood off the harpoon and used the blade, which he had sharpened on some flint, as a makeshift carving knife. And there we sat, in the still evening air, quietly chewing on the soft morsels of metallic flesh in some sort of abominable sea picnic. I tried to swallow my first piece but my weak yet morally sound stomach would not welcome it and I retched into the water. And there I watched the last part of my soul float away into the distance and I knew there was no way back for me.

The night passed slowly and we continued to eat the soft morsels of Andrew's flesh with shame. What had I done? It was becoming clear to me that I had now become a monster full of uncontrollable rage. I did not even know Andrew and yet I had taken his life. I considered that the least I could do was find out who my victim was and I asked Robert where he found him. So then the despicable scene played out of us discussing the life of our dinner. It turned out that Andrew had been born in a brothel but from the age of four he was raised by a priest who had patiently schooled him. The priest had brought Andrew to Robert and requested that he accompany our crew on our next voyage. The priest did not tell much of Andrew's story save that his mother's name was Kate and he was an avid reader, and he told Robert that Andrew had expressed a wish that he accompany myself on the ship, however, Robert could not guarantee how much contact he would have with me. Robert looked me square in the eyes and told me that following the mutiny Andrew specifically requested that he accompany us when we were cast away. I could hear Andrew's screams ringing in my ears as I was unwillingly dragged to the realisation that I had committed the ultimate sin and murdered my own flesh! I sat there motionless, eyes staring blankly ahead in dull shock. I could hear Robert and Blake trying to coax me out of my spell and I cannot tell how long I remained so.

Thoughts began to crowd my mind until they became a mass of shouting voices. I tried to pick out one thought to listen to or otherwise empty my mind entirely but it was no use and the tumult became louder still. I closed my eyes and pressed my hands to my forehead but the voices remained, so I reached over for the harpoon and began to press it into my chest. I had only managed a slight depression in my skin when Robert grabbed the blade and tried to snatch it from my hands. We tussled awhile however Robert's love for me and my instinct for self preservation were triumphant in the end, although as Robert pulled the blade back it gashed his leg severely. Although we managed to wrap Robert's leg with a cloth it was clear that without medical attention his leg would begin to rot.

The unquenchable thirst was the most painful experience any of us had ever endured, time was passing ever slowly and our aching heads could not withstand much more. Robert's leg was now rotting beyond all rescue but he could not endure the pain of hacking it off. Blake recounted to us a legend that he had heard where if the infected part of the leg turned a dark blue it was cursed and poisonous and would infect anyone who came into close proximity with it. This sounded like a myth to us, but in his feeble state and our situation, Blake was frightened of a painful and cursed death. Yet I hoped for it. I looked at Robert's leg praying for the black ooze to lighten its colour so that I may be poisoned and morph into a vacant ghost. But this did not happen and what eventually came instead was a cruel mockery of my pain.

All was quiet, my eyes were closed in deep meditation as I tried to dull the sharp hunger pains. Suddenly Blake let out a cry and pointed to the horizon. Robert and I, squinting, looked from Blake's pointed finger onward to see an imperceptible black dot. "Salvation!" we exclaimed. Hope. Tears were flowing down our cheeks, our tear ducts extravagantly not caring about our profound shortage of water. We yelped and screamed and loudly recited our prayers into the freezing air. We tried to draw the ship's attention to us and waited awhile until we were satisfied that the ship was indeed heading towards us. A heavenly floating sanctuary.

Soon the ship's grand shape was before us and at the helm stood a smiling man "Ahoy fellas, what brings you here?"

I stood up weakly in respect "My name is Captain Barnard of the Grampus. I report that there has been a mutiny aboard my ship and we have been cast away to survive the horrors of this untameable sea. We are hungry and weak and request your assistance."

"Well," replied the kindly Captain "I suppose y'all had better come on up"

A wave of gratitude swept over us as they let a rope ladder fall down into our welcoming hands. I ushered Robert forward and helped him place his decrepit leg onto the sturdy twine. As his trouser leg hitched up I noticed the faint hue of dark navy around his diseased calf. I held the rope weakly as he climbed up and then Blake eagerly reached for the ladder. As he did a gut wrenching screech reverberated across the ship as a voice shouted "Whale ahead!" Blake and I glanced to our right and sure enough a giant right whale was swimming straight towards our whale boat. Robert had got onto the ship and began a futile attempt to reach below desperately hoping that his stubby arm could reach us, but alas we still had our feet on the whale boat and could only look up in defeat. Blake panicked and flailed his arms against the ladder. But the feeling was there in our gut, the sickening realisation upon seeing our impending doom that we had no time. The ship's crew began to hurriedly steer the ship's course in the other direction and in doing so moved the ship away from our pitiful battered boat. Blake tried to hang onto the ladder but the coarse rope pulled away from his calloused hands and as the ship pulled away all we could do was wait for death.

But death did not come, the whale began to change course and navigated towards the sturdy ship, blocking it from us. We watched the whale drive the ship away towards the horizon. What a wretched turn of events! I could feel the anger rise up to my chest and I could have given anything to stab the rusting harpoon into the whale's bloated frame. I let out a sharp cry hoping to pierce its thick skin with my fury. Suddenly Blake exclaimed as he saw that the whale was now slowly creeping towards us. We braced ourselves for the inevitable. And yet.

The whale approached slowly until it stopped before us, almost as if it was observing our fearful expressions as we stood huddled together. And for what seemed like an eternity we each remained still, facing each other. All of a sudden I noticed four deep and perfectly symmetrical wounds in the whale's flesh. I half wondered whether my cries had caused them, but then I remembered this was the very same whale who crashed the Ivy. As I looked into its eyes I could sense the recognition. And in its final act of revenge it turned and swam away. I felt a crush of moral inferiority. How I had wronged the whale. How I had wronged Augustus and Andrew. I had felt their pulse in my hands and greedily drank their blood with no remorse, thinking only of my own colossal hunger. And now it is too late, they have gone leaving me here with heavy rocks of guilt so that I may teeter on the edge of drowning.

NB: This is a very interesting story, although it is patently clear that it can be nothing but a fragment of Inmate 325's imagination. For example, if Robert was rescued there would be a record of him or at the very least he would have made contact with Inmate 325, however when pressed about this Inmate 325 informs me that Robert did not make contact and he does not know what happened to him. Alternatively, if Blake's (highly questionable) theory of Robert's infected leg was true then the entire ship would have surely perished, which would have

resulted in some record. Furthermore, Blake and Inmate 325 would never have made it to land. I must say, he has a very vivid imagination.

Blake and I finished the remaining pieces of flesh which were not rotten and my throat greedily swallowed in spite of my revulsion. I studied Blake intently and noticed that he readily ate the flesh without remorse and indeed with some relish. I imagined that such cannibalism had altered his mind since the way in which he looked at me led me to believe that he thought me his next meal. I could swear when I looked into his eyes it was apparent that he was calculating whether my body would serve as a solid meal and whether my tepid blood would quench his thirst. Or they were perhaps my thoughts instead since we were both edging closer towards madness. After the corpse had rotted fully we lifted it out of the boat and watched it sink to the sea bed to its final and dignified resting place. Our thirst and hopelessness was overwhelming and we knew that it was only a matter of days before we were enveloped into the folds of merciful death. And still Blake was looking at me.

"What is it Blake?" He seemed to awake from some trance and apologised with embarrassment. "Talk to me" I instructed, "since we are to be each other's company in these final moments we must give each other strength. So talk to me"

"What about?" his eyes suddenly found new purpose as I put him to task.

I didn't know what about, but as I looked in his eyes I could see a peeping fox with countless secrets to tell. "Tell me something truthful ..... anything. Let's both exchange secrets" I don't know why but I needed some profound truth to chew on, to feed my hungry decrepit soul and choke on it.

Blake looked thoughtful "Ok ..... I was never married. I only told you I was married so you would think me a worthy man" I was smiling inside, it felt good, "I cheated on my wife" I said loudly into the air.

"I stole Andrew's pouch" he was becoming more animated and grinning slightly manically.

"Well, that's nothing, I stole his life" I was laughing hysterically with tears stinging my eyes.

"I knew he was your son from the beginning!", I stopped laughing and looked at him, eyes wide in surprise, "He told me on the ship. I didn't believe him at first but gradually he grew to be the very image of you."

I stared at him intently "Tell me about the mutiny Blake" I said quietly into the whispering breeze. His stupid grin had now disappeared and Blake narrowed his eyes in concentration "What?"

"The mutiny, tell me what happened. I wasn't there at the time, you reached it before me, so tell me about it?"

"Well" Blake took in a deep breath and fixed his eyes on the boat floor "there's nothing to tell ... the cook and Richard had planned the mutiny and started .... uh ... shouting at us to do what they said or ... or they would kill us. That's all that happened until you arrived, and you know the rest"

"That's very interesting Blake" I looked away into the distance "But as I recall you previously joined me in accusing Andrew of starting the mutiny". Blake continued to look at the boat floor and after a long pause he stammered "I ... I don't know what I said before, it feels like such a long time ago since so much has happened, I don't know, I don't remember".

I stared, unblinkingly, waiting for the realisation to come and yet I knew it was already with me. How could I have been so blind? How could I have missed the obvious and in the process taken the life of an accomplished scholar because of my insecurities and this snake tongued sailor. "So" the words barely escaping my parched lips "It was you", the silent world around me nodded yes and Blake's murmured denials floated away from me dissolving into the virtuously clear water.

Sometimes when so much has happened you feel empty, as if drained of all your strength, your ability to cope but also your ability to feel. In my eyes this must be deliberate. We must have been divinely created with some self preservation mechanism which immediately shuts down all feeling when the pain becomes too much to bear. And then you are left floating in the monstrous emptiness which you have created for yourself. And somehow you have not self destructed. Yet what a cursed creature am I that in reaching my lowest ebb not only have I failed to honourably depart into the nether, but I have dragged my trusted companion down to my level and drowned him so. And yet. Yet I still do not want to let go of the throbbing inside my chest, despite it all.

Perhaps because I have grown accustomed to the sick satisfaction in knowing I can sink no lower, it is a strange comfort indeed!

NB: Inmate pauses awhile in deep contemplation. I am not sure but I think I can see a slight twinkle in his eye. It seems that there is more to his theory. I suspect that he is a man who had lived a full life in his own imaginings and rather than not being able to let go of life he cannot let go of his dreams. For it is these that make up his life as he has sat here for years staring up at the ceiling. My diagnostic opinion is that he has classic symptoms of delusion.

And so we sailed on, Blake trying to lighten the mood with his infernal stories and me seething quietly to myself. I had decided that I would kill him. I decided this the moment I realised he had been the instigator of my misfortune, however, I lacked the strength and needed to save my energy until the opportune time presented itself. So I set about devising a strategy to topple his body and stab him with the rusting harpoon. Blake was, however, a little bigger than me and looked stronger. Indeed his low morals seemed to give him great outer strength not dissimilar to the inner strength displayed by Andrew's virtuous being. However, I now had the taste for blood having felt its pulsating energy in my hands and annihilated it into dust. I felt we were perfectly matched opponents, but as I calculated, the longer time passed the more favourable the conditions would be for him as he could retain more strength from food than I. So I had to move fast.

I awoke the next morning after a painfully disturbed sleep with an aching hunger and thirst and I resolved that now was the time. I knew that we would not be able to survive for much longer and it was now or never. There he slept, breathing slowly like a babe, and I climbed over to the edge of the boat and reached for the harpoon on the floor. As I got up and gradually moved towards him I could see behind him on the horizon a blurred dark line on the sea. I squinted slightly and then my weary hand released the harpoon which fell to the floor with a crash, waking Blake with a start. Both of us stood there, in numb stillness, as we floated towards land.

It is difficult to say what provoked me. Maybe it was stepping on land which loosed some faulty animal instinct which had thus far temporarily been buried. Maybe it was the jerk inside me upon seeing

Blake's smirking face as he turned and walked away from me. I do not know, yet before I realised what I was doing the townsfolk were pinning me down on the floor and pressing their clothes against Blake's gushing neck. I could hear the pattering of footsteps on the ground amongst the screaming and through it all I felt an immense release. The townsfolk must have thought it queer for this murderous being spread eagled on floor clawing at the earth and laughing to myself, which is probably why I was sent here. I told a few things to my first doctor, your predecessor, and he did what you're doing, muttering to himself and noting overly long words in his papers, and all the while leaving me to rot in my own misery. Which, in case you don't know the ending of my story, is exactly what you're going to do. But, nevertheless, that is certainly a weight off. It is the first time I have admitted how many people I had killed, and how many people I had failed, and now with this joyous relief in my confession I can sleep. I can now rest, in peace.

NB: At this Inmate 325 broke into a sad smile with tears running down his face. With his story complete he laid back and closed his eyes and drifted into a deep sleep. I tried to rouse him but I knew he would not say another word to me.

That ends my observation of Inmate 325, a vicious murderer with an extremely colourful imagination who is almost incapable of distinguishing between dream and reality. As such, my diagnosis is that he is suffering from extreme delusion and on occasion mild hysteria and I would recommend that he be committed to the psychiatric ward indefinitely or at the very least until the end of his sentence.

Report Ends.

… 6 months later …

The Doctor walked slowly down the street breathing in the cool morning air. A nonchalance about him and slight spring in his step, he seemed not to have a care in the world. He had consumed a delicious breakfast, kissed his wife and kids goodbye and was now thinking about his patients of the day. As a detour to his office he stopped by the newsstand to buy his usual daily newspaper. He read as he walked and slowly turned the pages. Towards the mid section of the paper he noticed a headline "Discovered – Manuscript of a mutiny". He read on and discovered that the unfinished manuscript was written by a sailor named Andrew Barnard of a mutiny which occurred on board the Grampus ship, "captained by Captain Barnard". The Doctor's eyes grew wide and the flailing sheets of the newspaper floated gently to the floor. Birds chirped, the cool breeze weaved between the people queuing up before the newsstand and the newspapers seller's voice blurred into the tapping of quickening footsteps.